Snap
Decision

Other books by Nathan Whitaker

Uncommon, by Tony Dungy with Nathan Whitaker

The Mentor Leader, by Tony Dungy with Nathan Whitaker

Quiet Strength, by Tony Dungy with Nathan Whitaker

Role of a Lifetime, by James Brown with Nathan Whitaker

Through My Eyes, by Tim Tebow with Nathan Whitaker

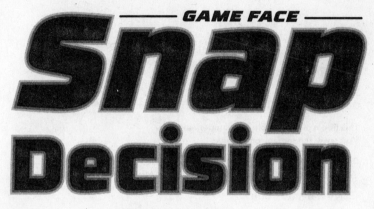

GAME FACE

Snap Decision

BOOK ONE

NATHAN WHITAKER

ZONDER**kidz**

ZONDERKIDZ

Snap Decision
Copyright © 2014 by Nathan Whitaker

This title is also available as a Zondervan ebook.
Visit www.zondervan.com/ebooks

Requests for information should be addressed to:
Zonderkidz, 3900 *Sparks Drive, Grand Rapids, Michigan* 49546

ISBN 978-0-310-73700-1

Published in association with the literary agency of Legacy, LLC, Winter Park, FL
32789.

Zonderkidz is a trademark of Zondervan.

Cover design: Kris Nelson
Cover illustration: Dave Phillips
Interior design: David Conn

Printed in the United States of America

14 15 16 17 18 19 /DCI/ 20 19 18 17 16 15 14 13 12 11 10 9 8 7 6 5 4 3 2 1

Dedication

To my mom, Lynda Whitaker, for passing along a joy of reading (and letting me hang out in your office with Dr. Carr).

CHAPTER 1

Chase looked at the game clock. Eighteen seconds left in the fourth quarter — in the entire game. They trailed by only four points with just those few seconds left. Winning was a long shot from their own 30-yard line, but it was still possible. Especially when it came to football.

They'd been down by ten against the Raiders at halftime, but now they were within a touchdown. Chase pictured himself lifted up by his teammates after pulling off a comeback win. The entire junior varsity team would be heroes at school tomorrow. Coach Skalaski would pull Chase aside and say, "*I knew you had it in you. We need your guts on varsity, Chase.*" Finally.

It all depended on this play.

Chase called the huddle and looked at the other ten faces. He tried to sound confident. "We need to make this work." He looked around the huddle. "We could win this." Chase's mind zipped through their regular plays. Coach Payne had let him call most plays, starting with the last game. He was trying to think about their options and not the fact that he was drenched with sweat and incredibly thirsty. He wiped his hands on his pants, but after almost four full quarters in the Florida sun, he didn't have a dry spot left. He reached over and dried his hands on the towel hanging from Solomon's pants.

Solomon turned, letting Chase use the towel.

"Chase likes rubbing his hands on your backside," said Nick, the shortest of the receivers. Solomon turned toward Nick, much taller and wider than Nick was. Letting the quarterback use his towel was one of Solomon's jobs as the center. The guys still liked to give Chase grief about that.

"I told you," Nick said. "Chase likes rubbing your backside."

Solomon turned toward Nick, and the look on Solomon's face said: Not. Another. Word. Solomon Williams was the ninth-grade center weighing 190 pounds at 5 feet 11 inches and could squash Nick Wood, shortest of the Loggerhead JV receivers who had yet to hit his post-pubescent growth spurt even though he was in ninth grade too. Nick wisely dropped it.

"Why don't we run a Go Route to my side?" asked Drew. Drew Ruiz, eighth-grader and perhaps their fastest receiver, twitched and jerked in anticipation, ready to run as the black paint dripped beneath his eyes from the heat.

"Pass to me," said Kris, the ninth-grade receiver with three inches on Drew. They had an ongoing competition for number of catches. Kris was currently in the lead, with eight receptions. "Drew may be fast, but under pressure he can't catch a cold."

But Drew packed some serious power. "You're just jealous of my fancy footwork. Especially since you have a girl's name," Drew said, and he shoved Kris's shoulder. Kris was tired of getting teased because of the way his parents spelled his name, but nearly keeled over anyway—despite his height. "You may be tall, but I still make you fall," Drew chanted.

Solomon was tall and wide, stocky but strong. Solid. He stood to his full height and glared down at Drew. Both Kris and Drew quieted down. They all focused on Chase.

"Seriously, guys," Chase said. "We could win this, and we need a win! I say we run *Trio Right Gun 200 Throwback.*"

He looked at the guys one-by-one. Solomon looked back at him through wet strands of sweaty black hair that hung down across his forehead. Drew looked determined, especially with the eye black. Kris looked exhausted but ready. Nick looked sick. Carson looked scared. His eyes were wide. Really wide.

"It's on you, Carson," Chase said.

Carson took a deep breath, and his look of fear turned to resolve. His eyes narrowed and he nodded. He knew what was expected of him.

"We can do this," Chase said.

"You can do it, Chase!" boomed JB from the sidelines, as if on cue.

Solomon snickered. "Did you pay him to do that?"

James Brown, star senior varsity quarterback, sitting in the nearly empty bleachers next to Tripp, Chase's long-time best friend. JB was actually cheering for Chase, eighth-grader quarterbacking the JV team. What Chase would give to be sitting with them as a member of the varsity team, cheering on the JV instead of running plays for the "little guys." If Chase ever had a chance of playing varsity soon, he figured he'd better get it together now.

"See, guys, even JB thinks so. Let's do it! *Trio RightGun 200 Throwback*! On two!" Chase reminded himself to focus. But still, JB *knew* his name?

Wow! Chase thought.

Focus!

"Loggerheads!" they called and broke the huddle, racing into formation. The Loggerheads were seventy yards away from the Raiders' end zone. That play was their only hope. A tough throw and catch, especially for JV, but Coach Preston had taught them the varsity plays so every football player in the school, no matter what level, would be using the same system. They were smaller and younger than the varsity players, so it would be tougher. Chase couldn't throw it anywhere near seventy yards, so Carson would have a long run after the catch.

Definitely tougher, but they could do it. *He* could do it. Right? *Focus.*

They lined up on the ball in the shotgun formation with Chase several steps behind Solomon. The *Gun* part of the play call. Chase stood and called the cadence, "Blue 17, Blue 17, Hut, Hut!" He almost always called "Blue 17," but he didn't know why, it just sounded good. *On two* meant that he would say "hut" twice, after which Solomon would snap the ball.

Chase caught the snap, and ran to his right to buy time for his three receivers. *Trio Right*—Nick, Drew, and Kris—ran straight down the right side of the field, as fast as possible, distracting the defense, while Carson, the fourth receiver, ran straight toward the middle goalpost, toward the Raiders' end zone, then he cut left for the *Throwback*—the key to the play. While Chase and everyone else ran right, Carson was cutting to the left. Chase scanned the field, watching for Carson to cut left. He was almost there!

Chase danced back and forth, narrowly missing a Raider's tackle. *Wait for it,* he thought. *Nearly there...* Carson angled toward the sideline. *Now!*

"Look out!" Tripp's voice reached Chase's ears over the sounds of the small crowd.

Look out for what? Chase thought. And then, *Wham!*

He was slammed to the ground by the Raiders' defensive end from behind on his left. Blind-sided!

Chase felt his body hit the ground — hip, shoulders, head. He felt the ball pop from his hands, and saw it hit the turf, quickly covered by a pile of colors, the blues and greens of his team, and grays and reds of the Raiders.

It didn't matter what team recovered the ball. Time had run out. There'd be no more plays in this game.

Fumble. Game over. The Loggerheads lost.

Again.

CHAPTER 2

Chase sat in the back row of first-period Algebra I honors class with Tripp. Tripp folded a piece of notebook paper into an origami football, shook his mop of blond hair out of his eyes, and flicked the football toward the front of the class. Score! It hit Hannah smack in the back of her head. Chase's sister glanced over her shoulder and rolled her eyes.

Hannah was almost a full year older than Chase and in the same grade, which was no big deal except that she got annoyed when people perpetually pegged them as twins. "I'm older," she would quickly point out.

Chase and Hannah got along well, for the most part. They were aces when it came to academics and studied together more often than not, but they drew the line at sitting next to each other in class.

Hannah was always in the front row anyway, usually next to Megan Brown, like she was now.

"Megan Brown?" the substitute teacher called out.

"Here," Megan responded. Megan was Hannah's best friend since second grade, JB's little sister ... and kicker for Loggerheads varsity — the only girl on the team, ever.

"Chase Clark?"

"Here," Chase answered. Thank God it came out right. Two weeks ago, his voice started cracking, and ever since then Chase had been thinking thirteen wasn't such a good age.

Chase had seamlessly and uneventfully passed from one grade to the next at Archie F. Carr School. He'd been here since the second grade and would likely finish high school here. It was the only community school serving all of Lincoln, Florida, boasting a population of 20,000 residents.

So far, his first month or so of eighth grade had been enjoyable, typical, until the voice thing showed up. It had happened last week during morning attendance; Chase called out, "Here!" and his voice cracked so hard it sounded like a chalkboard squeaking. It seriously went up two octaves within a single one-syllable word, halfway through. The entire class laughed, and Chase was mortified.

Since then, Chase avoided raising his hand in class. Hopefully, this voice thing would pass quickly. So far, this day was off to a good start.

Mrs. Wright was a regular substitute at Carr. After attendance, she told the class, "Pick up reading where you left off and do the problems at the end of the chapter on factorials." Then Mrs. Wright looked at Hannah and asked, "Would you come up here, please, Hannah?"

Hannah stood and walked up to the teacher's desk. Chase leaned over to talk to Tripp, not only his best friend but also his next-door neighbor. All the Clarks had liked the Stevens family from the first time they'd met six years ago, when they were looking at buying the house next door. At the time, Mrs. Clark was just divorced, moving from Atlanta with her two children, Chase and Hannah, back to her childhood hometown in North Florida.

Tripp and Chase had done everything together since they moved in. Now, they whispered together as they watched Hannah walk to the front.

Hannah often wore blue shirts, and today it was one of her light ones, a powdery sky blue shade. She was right, Chase thought, the blues always looked good against her light brown hair and blue eyes. Hannah and Mrs. Wright spoke quietly for a moment, while Chase and the other students looked on. Tripp leaned over and whispered to Chase again.

"I'm glad I'm not Hannah. I don't have to teach Mrs. Wright the lesson every time she shows up."

Chase nodded and grinned. "The drawback to being

the smartest kid in class. Fortunately, *you* won't ever have to worry."

Tripp punched Chase's shoulder and said, "As I recall, I beat you with a 98 on the last test."

"Ow!" Chase said, massaging his shoulder. "Relax!"

Mrs. Wright looked up. They immediately dropped their eyes. It would be an easy class as long as they stayed quiet.

A while later Chase whispered, "That's nothin'! What was it I got in history? Was that a perfect 100 percent? *So there.*"

Mrs. Wright nailed Chase with another glare prompting him to bury his head in his math book.

Tripp put pencil to paper and started plugging away at the algebra equations. Chase had finished these problems yesterday. He liked staying ahead of his homework, and math came easy for him.

Definitely easier than, say, English, where he did okay but had to work a lot harder. Chase started zoning out and stared at the portrait of Archie F. Carr, perched above the blackboard.

Lincoln was a small town in northern Florida, midway between Jacksonville and Gainesville. Founded after the Civil War, it was a farming community that raised a lot of cattle and peanuts. When the wind blew the wrong way, *lots* of cattle. At first, the school had first been called River County High. It didn't become the Archie F. Carr School until 1990, after Carr, a world-renowned zoologist, had died. Professor Carr had been a longtime University of Florida sea turtle researcher.

Eventually, the school was renamed the Archie F. Carr School, and so the loggerhead sea turtle became the school's official mascot. Over time, there had been talk of building a separate elementary school, but Lincoln quit growing and the little kids stayed on campus with the older kids.

So that's how it was that most of the people from Lincoln had grown up attending the same school, in a town that stayed small enough that everyone knew most everyone else. Carr students, staff and parents shared a feeling of pride in the Carr Loggerheads. They shared a sense of legacy, of family.

The bell went off, snapping Chase out of his town-history trance. As he and Tripp joined the mass of students leaving the classroom, Chase once again felt dwarfed by the 5-foot – 10-inch Tripp. He'd shot up six inches over the summer, and Chase saw the difference at random times, like when they were bouncing into each other in the bustling hallway.

Chase spotted Coach Preston coming out of the classroom. Coach called out, "Hey, Chase, got a minute?"

"Sure," Chase said. He turned to Tripp. "See ya, Thug."

"Yup. See ya, Thug," he echoed and headed to his next class.

"Nice words of endearment there," Coach Preston said.

Chase's ears burned. "It's, uh, just something we made up awhile back."

"Whatever you say," Coach said. Chase liked Coach Preston. Coach had missed the second game of the season because his wife was having a baby. Rumor had it the baby girl was born right at kickoff. She was now only weeks old, and her name was Elise, but the players knew her as "Kickoff."

"What class do you have next? I'll walk with you."

"Science," Coach nodded as they walked side by side.

Coach Preston, or "Coach P," was one of the Carr football coaches. Coach Skalaski was head of the entire football program and varsity coach, and Coach Quinn, who'd joined the faculty two years ago, when he got out of college, worked with the varsity, too. Coach Preston, junior varsity head coach, was also *Mr.* Preston, or "Mr. P," American history teacher. Chase quickly determined Preston was in coach mode, not teacher stance. He had a seriousness that was wrapped in football energy.

Was this about last night's game? Chase knew he had messed up that last play, even though he'd tried his best.

Instead, Coach P said, "I want to apologize for yelling last night."

"It's okay," Chase said. It hadn't been that bad, actually. Chase only remembered him yelling once.

"No, no," Coach P said. "Coach Skalaski has clear standards, and one is no yelling at you guys or the refs — I respect that. I plan to tell the rest of the team at practice." Coach P looked uncomfortable.

They arrived at the classroom, and Chase stood with Coach Preston outside the door. Hopefully, this wouldn't take long. Chase felt the stares of his classmates. He noticed Kate Newman, looking at him as she walked through the door.

Immediately, Chase's face felt as hot as a day at the beach in Florida's July sun. Kate Newman, of the long blonde hair and deep brown eyes. He quickly looked away and back at Coach P.

"Coach Skalaski would like more wins, but at the JV level he's more interested in making sure you are improving and learning the plays, preparing players for varsity."

Chase's heart raced at the mere mention of playing varsity. From talking to Tripp, he knew a lot about the expectations of varsity's head coach. He couldn't wait for his chance to prove himself worthy.

"You make a good effort, and you're a good leader," Coach P said. "Coach Skalaski and I both think you have a shot at getting called up this season."

Did I just hear that? Chase wanted to shout *Yes! Yes!*

Yes! But he kept his composure as other kids moved steadily past.

"Anyway, get into class. I'll see you at practice."

Chase was the last to slip into science class, where he would have a hard time switching his attention from football to protons. He couldn't wait to tell Tripp.

It had been the end of August when Chase burst into Tripp's room and told him the news. "You made it!" Chase had said. He high-fived, shouted at the right times, and was genuinely happy for Tripp. He really was. Except he did wish Tripp didn't have early morning workouts sometimes, so they could still ride their bikes to school together.

Tripp was cool about it and didn't rub it in. He was excited, but almost seemed embarrassed. It was really unusual for an eighth grader to make the team at the start of the year. But there had been a strange buzzing in Chase's ear all afternoon, and he couldn't help thinking, *Why couldn't it have been me?*

But that's the way it worked for the Archie F. Carr School football program. All grades attended one building, there wasn't a freshman team, and every student could play every sport, at any level, if they proved up to it. It happened more in baseball or volleyball, but rarely in football.

There was flag football in elementary, and a decent middle-school team for fifth through seventh grades, even if they sometimes had to combine with other schools to have enough players.

But the high school varsity team took the best players after summer workouts and left the rest to play junior varsity, mostly eighth- and ninth-graders. It might be a year or two, even three, before some players moved up to varsity — if ever.

But, occasionally, an eighth grader would make varsity, like Mark Plazas had. Probably Carr's greatest athlete, he'd played at Carr ten years earlier, had been an All-American at the University of Texas, and still played every Sunday in the NFL.

Megan and Tripp were the first eighth-graders to make it in a long time. Maybe this message from Coach P meant Chase was finally on his way up. He hoped so.

CHAPTER 3

Chase found Tripp at lunch at the varsity table. Tripp slid over to make room for Chase and someone yelled, "No JV scrubs!" Chase ignored it and scooted in. No one else said anything, but Chase couldn't help feeling as if all eyes were upon him.

"Hey, Chase." It was Chris Kingston. Chase knew Chris and his twin brother Will, both juniors and varsity offensive linemen. They were second-generation Chinese-American, which was pretty different in Lincoln. They had a fan following, mostly girls, but really, everyone liked the Kingstons.

Besides them, Chase knew a couple others at the table — Roger Dalton, backup quarterback to JB, and Jackson Parker, another receiver. *Sophomore*, Chase thought. He knew *of* Dimitri Anderson and Walker Skinner, but they'd never officially met. Collectively, they looked more like a group of high-school footballers at church rather than a bunch of kids about to engage in a typical cafeteria lunch. Button-down shirts and ties weren't required but were common on gameday. Chase had looked the same yesterday. JV played on Thursdays, varsity on Fridays.

"Tough game last night, Chase," said Will.

"Yeah, the Raiders were pretty good. They had some really tough defensive players. And we're" — Chase paused — "not so good." He shrugged sheepishly.

"You almost won," said Roger. "Came down to the wire. It could have gone either way." Roger Dalton was a senior and had bleach-blond surf's-up hair and "dreamy-blue" eyes, according to Hannah. Chase's sister had swooned over Roger since fifth grade.

"Yeah, Tripp tried to save me by yelling on that last play, but … oh, well. Maybe if the heads-up came a bit sooner, I could've made it."

"Keep telling yourself that," Tripp said. "Whatever gets you through the night."

"You all should come and cheer us on, next game …" Chase trailed off as he realized he'd just told a table of varsity football players what to do. He loved that he got to sit with them, but he knew it was only because of Tripp, so maybe he shouldn't push it.

"Yeah, good luck with that," Dimitri laughed.

"Can it!" Will said. "You remember what it was like

to be one of the little guys. Give him a break." The table erupted in laughter.

"Seriously, though. I've noticed your defense seems to be tightening up," Will said. "Everyone on your offensive line is getting better. And that Solomon Williams guy — he's a bus! He'll be a force to be reckoned with before long."

"Wow, who knew one of varsity's players paid so much attention to JV?" Chase said.

Will shrugged. "I'm always watching," he said. "Learn and adapt. That's how I roll."

"I surf. That's how I roll," said Roger. Chase couldn't tell if he was being a jerk or not.

Chase reddened anyway, and turned back toward Will. "I could use some pointers anytime," Chase said.

Tripp clapped him on the back. "My man's been *awesome*!"

Chase could feel himself starting to sweat. Tripp could give him all the props he wanted, but Chase knew no matter how good he played, at this point varsity already had two quarterbacks, both seniors — JB and Roger.

"So what do you think about Senior Skip Day this year?" Will asked the group.

"What about it?" Dimitri asked.

"Who's in? Or should I say 'out'?"

The boys started buzzing about the annual senior-class tradition of designating a day to ditch school. *Who'd get caught? Who'd get grounded?* Roger and

Dimitri were both skipping, from what Chase gathered. But then he saw Kate Newman walk by to join Hannah and Megan at a nearby table. Chase followed her with his eyes, barely registering Roger, Chris, and Dimitri as they detailed their plans for Skip Day.

Tripp leaned over. "I heard Kate will be studying with Hannah and Megan this weekend."

"Uh, great," Chase said. He tried to act like this intel didn't affect him at all, but his mind was already leafing through his homework to-do list for something they could study as a group.

Tripp looked at him, smirking.

"What?" Chase said, trying not to smile.

The last three periods of classes dragged by. It was Friday and he didn't have a game, so they didn't go by quickly at all.

That night, Chase's mom drove Hannah and him ten minutes around the woods to the Carr stadium for the varsity football game against Palatka High School. Carr's varsity was 5 – 0 and was expected to have an easy win that night against the Palatka Panthers. Chase, Hannah, and their mom found Tripp's parents in the stands, which wasn't too hard, since the Stevens arrived early to watch Tripp in pregame warmups, and sat in the same spot every week.

Tripp's dad grinned. "How's it going, Guy?" and gave Chase a fist bump. Chase sat next to him, while Hannah and her mom started talking with Mrs. Stevens.

"Pretty well," said Chase. "School's been fine, and football has been pretty good too. Of course, we've only won one game."

"Yeah, I wished I'd made it last night. I was at the University of Alabama and didn't get in until late this afternoon. Tripp said you did well, and honestly, you guys don't need to get too worried about winning and losing right now. You're so young and still learning the game. Learn to play it right."

Chase nodded. Mr. Stevens, a scout for the NFL team, the Jacksonville Destroyers, had told him that many times. "The most important thing you can do is to try and keep improving. At your age, that's what you need to do. I mean, you haven't even played football very long." Chase had started playing quarterback only that year, but had a pretty strong arm for an eighth-grader, and a young eighth-grader at that.

Chase nodded.

They turned their attention toward the field. The varsity squad of Loggerheads was coming out of the locker room in their blue and green uniforms, and broke through a giant paper sign the cheerleaders were holding up at the edge of the field. They ran to their sideline, jumping up and down until the entire team had arrived. Everyone cheered. Tripp looked up at them and gave a small wave, his hand down by his hip. Saying "hey" while still being cool.

Chase could feel Mr. Stevens look at him and turned.

Mr. Stevens smiled, a smile that went all the way to his eyes. "You're just like I was, Chase. Don't get frustrated. Be anxious for nothing."

Chase nodded. "It's just hard," he sighed.

"I know. I've told you, that's exactly how I was. I was younger than the other guys in my grade. So I was smaller for my age than they were. I didn't catch up until I was *leaving* high school."

Chase remembered. Mr. Stevens had told him this before, but still, it was hard to imagine sometimes. Mr. Stevens wore a big green Loggerheads jacket and filled it out pretty well. It was hard to imagine him as small and skinny.

"You've just got to give it time. You'll catch up. Keep learning. You're a good athlete."

Chase felt relieved. He was glad Mr. Stevens lived next door.

As they watched the game there was plenty of cheering to be done, especially when Tripp's number 82 was called for a play. Carr did, in fact, have an easy time putting away the Panthers, and ended up beating Palatka 34 – 7, for their sixth win in a row to start the season.

After the game Chase and the others waited for Tripp. It was a perfect Florida night, slightly cool and dry, great for sleeping out in their tree house. Chase wondered if Tripp would be up for it. They hadn't done it since summer. He and Tripp had built the tree house the summer after Chase moved to Lincoln, when they were both eight, with the help of Mr. Stevens.

Tripp appeared, showered and shouldering his gym bag. He walked over to Chase. "Sorry I'm so late getting here," Tripp said. "There was, uh, a lot of celebrating."

"It's cool," Chase said, though he was feeling left out. "It might be cool to sleep in the tree house tonight. You up?"

"Actually, I'm sorry, Chase. There's an after-party for the team at Coach Skalaski's and ..."

"No, I got it," Chase said. Mr. and Mrs. Stevens came up behind Tripp. Mom and Hannah were right behind them.

"Going out?" Mr. Stevens asked.

"Yeah, if that's okay with you ..."

"I'll need to talk to Coach about how late you'll be, but it should be fine," Mr. Stevens said.

Tripp looked back at Chase. He was uncomfortable, and the moment grew awkward.

"Definitely, go," Chase said, disguising how left out he actually felt for Tripp's sake. On the ride home, for once, Chase was glad for Hannah's nonstop chatter. He thought again of the tree house, and the night he and Tripp stayed out watching the Perseid meteor shower. It was late August — Chase remembered because it was colder than usual for that time of year, and he and Tripp had buried deep in their sleeping bags. They were trying to count all the shooting stars. They'd lost track after thirty-five.

"I have a crazy idea," Tripp had said.

"Uh-oh, watch out."

"You know how hugging's not cool for guys? How girls hug anyone, anytime, even perfect strangers. But for guys it's just not cool?"

"I guess," Chase said.

"So how 'bout instead of hugging or fist-bumping or whatever, we could say something like, 'See ya, Thug,' and only you and I will know what it means."

"See ya, Thug?" Chase almost laughed, but he saw Tripp was serious.

"Yeah. See ya, Thug."

CHAPTER 4

"I'm tired of studying," Chase said. He yawned and stretched his arms overhead. Daisy took that as a signal to jump in his lap and lick his face, but Chase gently shooed the yellow Labrador retriever back to the ground. Tripp, Chase, Hannah, and Megan were studying for Monday's science test. Hoping Kate was coming over, Chase had suggested a group study session. Turned out Kate had to babysit her younger siblings and couldn't make it.

"Let's keep at it — we're almost done," Hannah said. "Just this science worksheet, then tomorrow we won't have anything."

"It's just as well," Megan said. "I can't do any more. It's gorgeous outside!"

"Yeah, our whole Saturday afternoon has been

inside," Chase said. "I don't think Mom will care if we cut our study time short."

Mom spent a lot of Saturdays at her office. This day, she had to prepare for a case going to trial on Monday. Before the divorce, Mrs. Clark hadn't used her University of Washington law degree while living in Atlanta, where their father was a trial attorney. After the divorce, she'd moved near her parents in Florida, to her hometown of Lincoln, and went to work in Gainesville as an attorney.

"Come on," Hannah urged, waving the paltry homework paper in the air, demonstrating its inability to intimidate. "We can knock this thing out in no time."

Tripp and Chase were reluctant, but the four tag-teamed their way through the study sheet and within thirty minutes, they were shooting baskets in front of Tripp's house. Tripp and Hannah vs. Chase and Megan.

Megan had long legs and was tall for the eighth grade, almost as tall as Tripp, and towered over Chase and Hannah. She was also the kicker for the varsity football team. Like most high schools, Carr had never had a girl on the football team, and Megan became the first. It didn't hurt that JB was her older brother — or that she was really good. When Coach Skalaski saw her kick before the season, he hadn't thought twice. She was on the team.

The basketball games were pretty even, and the kids played until they were worn out.

By then, Chase's mom was home, and the rest of the day went by quietly.

Until that night, when woofing sounds bounced off the kitchen walls. No, it wasn't Daisy begging for more bacon, but Chase's ringtone: *"Who-who-who-who-who? Who let the dogs out? Who-who-who-who-who? ..."*

Chase picked up his cell phone. "Hello?"

"Hey, buddy! How's my guy?"

"Dad! How are you?" Chase slipped into his room, in case his mom heard him.

"Good. Really good, Sport. How are you?"

"I'm doing great! It's football season, you know. I've been playing pretty well, and ..."

"Funny you should mention football, Chase. I've got a client who lives in Detroit, and I want to get him tickets for the Detroit-Jacksonville game in Detroit next month, and I know Mr. Stevens might be able to get good seats."

"Right." Chase's excitement faded.

"I mean, I'll pay for them, of course. I just don't want my client to have to sit in the last row or anything, you know? So you'll ask Tripp's dad about it? I could call him, but I really wanted to talk to you."

"No, sure. I'll ask him."

"Great, thanks! So you're doing well?"

"I really am! I'm still on JV, but Coach P says ..."

"That's great, Chase, really great. I'm proud of you. When's the next game?"

"It's—" Chase started, but his dad was interrupted by a voice in the background.

"What? I'll be right there. Hey, I'm sorry, I've got to go. I'm at a work conference. Please tell Hannah I love her and text me your game schedule. And give me a call when you hear about those tickets, okay?"

"Okay, Dad."

"Love you, Chase."

"Love you, too."

Sunday morning was busy, but fun. Bacon and eggs shared with Daisy, a Sunday trip to church, more basketball and football in the yard, and video games with Tripp. They'd been outside all weekend between the two houses. Both families lived in fairly small, simple homes, with huge yards of about three acres each. A great place to play baseball or football, but a lousy place when it was time to mow. Because the yards were adjoining, Tripp and Chase usually took turns on Mr. Stevens' riding mower.

That afternoon, Chase and Tripp were sitting on the couch eating pretzels for a break with Kayla, Tripp's sister, when Tripp's mom walked into the room.

"Oh, Mom. Chase's dad called last night," Tripp said.

"Is that right?" his mom asked.

Tripp nodded. Chase beamed.

Tripp's mom took a slow breath then smiled. "I'm really glad." But she didn't sound really glad, even as she said it.

Chase worried that the Stevens thought his dad didn't call or visit enough. "He'd call more if he could. But he's just a very busy guy. Atlanta's a very busy town," Chase said.

Mrs. Stevens smiled. "Of course. It's not that we don't *like* your dad – "

"Dad can't stand him," Kayla chimed in. "Really! I heard him once!" Kayla was ten and said pretty much whatever came into her head. "Dad says he never calls or visits, unless it's a birthday, or he needs something."

"He just called to say hi," Chase said. "And he wanted to talk to Mr. Stevens sometime, he said. He had a question about the Destroyers." Chase found himself unable to tell the rest of the conversation about the tickets. He was torn. His dad never showed up or called. Well, hardly, but at the same time, he liked him. After all, he was *his dad.*

Tripp's mom smiled. "Boys, *you* guys need to go see a professional game with Tripp's dad sometime soon. I think you guys would have a really good time."

"I love going to games in Jacksonville," said Chase.

"No, somewhere else. A road trip," said Mrs. Stevens.

"That'd be so cool!" Chase yelled.

Tripp grinned. "It really is fun," he told Chase.

"I want to go too," Kayla whined.

"You get to go plenty. This'll just be a boys' trip," Mrs. Stevens responded. Kayla pushed her lower lip out in a pout. "You're right, it's not fair. But that's just how this time will be. Remind us to call your mom, Chase, to get it on her calendar for you to go."

Tripp nodded. "See ya, Thug."

"See ya, Thug."

Chase raced home to tell his mom about the game.

Chase didn't ever have to eat breakfast alone, thanks to Daisy. Monday morning was no different, after studying and playing all weekend. Chase didn't mind. Neither did Daisy, who nuzzled his leg and stared at him with her big, dark eyes.

"Just one more, Daisy. One of these days, you're going to get us caught." Chase slipped another piece of bacon to the dog. Her third piece of the four Chase's mom had set out for his breakfast. Daisy wasn't nearly as interested in the scrambled eggs. And he doubted she was really fine stopping at three — but he'd already eaten the other, before she could nuzzle him again. Self defense, defending his bacon. Fast eating.

And they'd already been caught, plenty of times. It had become a family joke, the idea that Daisy only ate dog food. Well, she only ate dog food except for *all* of the other food that she ate from the table that Chase, Hannah, and their mom handed down to her. Especially bacon. Daisy's eyes didn't look worried about the chances of being found out.

"Okay, girl, I gotta go." Chase stood and headed toward his bedroom.

The yard was huge and the house wasn't, but it worked. Chase and Hannah had their own bedrooms, even though they had to share a bathroom. Chase heard Hannah turn the shower off, just before Mom came racing into the kitchen.

"Don't even try it," Mom said to Daisy. "How many bacon strips have you had already? Three? Four?" She turned off the coffee maker, then swiftly stacked dishes in the sink. "Hannah, I'm about to walk out!"

Chase cleared his place and put his dishes in the dishwasher. Daisy looked at him with sad eyes — *that's it?* — and then laid down in disappointment. Plus, she was tired. She'd been awake for twenty whole minutes now, the same as Chase.

His mom practiced law by herself and wasn't with other lawyers in a firm, so she always dressed nicely in case a client showed up at the office. Of course, she didn't spend much time in court, so it wasn't often that she had to dress up a lot, either. Just nice, every day. Chase's only concern was choosing clean clothes.

"You look nice, Mom," Chase said, and she did. She was wearing a dressier skirt and suit jacket than her usual office attire. "You're looking quite professional."

"Thanks, Chase," she said, stopping for a moment to really look at him. "Come here and give me a hug."

"No," Chase said. "That's gross," but he leaned toward her anyway.

"You're a fine young man," she said as she gave Chase a loving squeeze around his shoulders. "Now get going, or you'll be late!"

Hannah poked her head into the kitchen and said, "Have at it, Chase."

"'Bout time," he said, heading to the bathroom.

A room for him and one for Hannah, and a bathroom that they shared. Plus a room and bathroom for their mom. They didn't have overnight guests often, but when they did, Hannah stayed with their mom and the guests took Hannah's room, which was always neat and tidy.

He brushed his teeth, and his mom stuck her head in one last time. "Have a great day. Do you have lunch money?"

Foam spilled out of his mouth as he tried to answer, but she was already out the door. She always asked, even though she knew that he'd made sure the night before. Hannah was right behind her, catching a ride to school before his mom headed to her office thirty minutes away in Gainesville.

He still had three minutes if he was going to beat Hannah, which he tried to do most days. For no reason, just to prove that his bike was faster than their car. He let Daisy out and back in, finished his teeth, ran a hand through his wet, dark brown hair, grabbed his backpack off his desk and looped it over his shoulder.

He raced his bike down the driveway they shared with Tripp's house, around the corner, and turned left onto the bike path. From there, it was a straight shot to Carr, which was really right behind their house "as the crow flies," as Gramps liked to say. Because of the thick woods between their house and the school, his mom always insisted that he stay on the bike path. It was longer but quicker than walking straight through the woods, and far shorter than driving. His mom and Hannah had to take two left turns and go through several lights, but now that Hannah was in eighth grade, she didn't want to take a chance of sweating before school.

Chase didn't mind, and raced up the path, Carr looming in front of him.

That afternoon, Chase and his teammates were back at practice. In the rain.

The ball slipped out of Chase's hand as he threw it, and it flittered off to the side and fell to the ground nowhere near anyone. Chase groaned.

Coach Preston yelled, "That's the fourth one today!"

Some guys love playing in the rain, especially defensive guys. Chase didn't. His hands were small but still growing, he hoped, so rain made hanging on to the ball that much tougher for him. Chase decided he wasn't a big fan of rain. Practices were harder, plus he and Tripp had to mow more often.

Otherwise, he actually liked practice. He had a

surprisingly strong arm, at least that's what people said. He hadn't played much football at all before this season — baseball had always been his first love — but he was learning quickly and felt that he was improving with every single practice. But rain was another story.

"I wish it would just start pouring," muttered Chase.

"No kidding," said Solomon. "I'd much rather go to the gym than be out in this."

When it rained hard enough, Coach Skalaski sent his players inside and often told Coach Preston to bring the JV in too. Chase could see the varsity over on their field, practicing, and unfortunately it wasn't raining so hard that they had to go inside. The coaches tried to stay outside if they could, because the gym wasn't wide enough to run the plays that they wanted to practice. It was far too small to send the defense to one side and the offense to another like they did outside, and it really got squeezed when the varsity *and* JV were in there together. So it was only as a last resort Coach took them inside — and this was not a last resort.

"On second thought, let's just quit throwing the ball today," Coach Preston said. "Only running plays from here on out. But when we're done here, Chase, I want you doing wet ball drills."

As if the rain wasn't bad enough. With wet ball drills, Coach Preston made him use old rubber balls dunked in water. Coach Preston said that Carr couldn't afford to ruin their practice balls, so he insisted on the rubber balls, which were already pretty slippery. Water made them completely impossible for Chase to hold, and yet somehow, Coach Preston's drills would supposedly help him improve in case they ever had a game in the rain.

Finally, practice ended, and the rest of the team left for the locker room, but Chase headed toward the bucket and the rubber footballs waiting for him.

Dunk. Snap. Step back and throw. Then dunk the next ball, take the snap, step and throw. Over and over. He was quickly bored, but then thought back to Mr. Stevens' words: keep learning. Keep improving.

Chase turned back toward the bucket and balls with new purpose. He looked over at the varsity practice field once more and broke out in a huge grin as he saw Tripp's number eighty-two jersey flash down the sideline. The brightly colored varsity practice jerseys flashed blue and green, so much better than the hand-me-down JV practice jerseys. *How great it would be to wear the varsity jerseys, even in practice*, Chase thought.

Twenty minutes later, Chase was leaving the field at long last, heading for the locker room. He didn't think any of his teammates would still be there. As he ran off, he saw that the varsity guys were heading off their field too, toward the locker room they all shared.

Chase ended up trotting in with the varsity guys, laughing with Tripp and Will when he spotted Tripp's helmet.

"Whoa. Is that new?" The helmet was sleek, with an extra ribbon of plastic down the middle.

Tripp nodded. "Yeah. The new Riddell. Coach passed them out to the specialty players — running backs, quarterbacks, wide receivers. They're worried about concussions."

"Man, that looks cool."

"Yeah, I just hope it works. They said that if you get a concussion from now on, you have to sit out at least two games — maybe more — before they will let you play."

"Wow."

"Yeah, wow," said Tripp. "They aren't messing around, Coach said." Just then, Chase heard a voice right beside him, on his other side. "Chase, can I talk to you?" Chase turned.

Coach Skalaski stood behind him. Chase's heart missed a beat.

"Uh, sure, Coach." Chase stopped and the guys called out their goodbyes as they continued. Could this be it? He'd played okay, but they'd only won one game so far, and Chase *was* the quarterback. He thought back to Coach Preston's talk with him. Or was he in trouble?

"I wanted to give you a heads up," Coach Skalaski said, then put his concerns to rest. "I'm looking to have you fill in on the varsity team, possibly as early as next game. Something may be coming up. We may be shorthanded."

"Uh, okay," Chase said. Had he heard right? After the practice he'd just had? "I'm happy to help anytime. I'll do whatever you want."

Coach gave his shoulder a friendly pat. "I know you will," he said. "You're a good kid. I'll let you know as soon as possible whether I'll need you for the game, maybe early next week."

They walked into the locker room together, and Coach spotted Chase's teammate, Solomon, just walking out of the other door. "Solomon, wait!" he called. Coach turned back to Chase. "You've done good work, son. I'll let you know."

Chase found Tripp in the locker room, and told him the news quietly so none of the other guys would hear. He didn't want to hurt anyone's feelings or seem like he was bragging. It took every ounce of energy for Chase *not* to grab Tripp in a bear hug, chest bump, jump up and down, and run screaming through the locker room.

"Yes!" Tripp said. "I knew it was a matter of time. You've got agility and a great arm, we're gonna rock this team!"

"Let me tell your dad. I'll come over after dinner."

"It's your news," Tripp said. "But hurry, because I won't be held accountable if I slip up and mention it."

The boys raced home on their bikes, making it in record time. The sun was setting as Chase walked through the door.

"I'm home!" Chase hollered.

42

"In the kitchen," Mom answered.

His mom, Cindy, with her dark curly hair and her slight build, always seemed so young. He'd always liked having a young mom.

"What's got you in such a good mood?" she asked, smiling. She was always smiling.

"Coach said I might get called up to varsity next week." His mom cheered and leapt across the kitchen to give him a hug. The noise brought Hannah out of her room. When she heard the news, she cheered and high-fived Chase, and so did Megan, who'd been studying with Hannah in her room too.

That night they celebrated over dinner — the four of them.

"Did Coach tell you when it would happen?" Hannah asked.

"No, and it may not even happen at all," he answered. "He went over and talked to Solomon after me, and I'm guessing it was about the same thing. I was going to text Solomon, and then I thought maybe he hadn't, and I didn't want to bring it up and look like I was bragging."

Chase's mom agreed.

"So, I guess I'll just wait and see."

Dinner ended, and the kids were thankful they didn't have any algebra homework. That was the one bright spot of having a substitute for four days — that Hannah had to teach about the lesson plans.

Chase ran next door to the Stevens' house.

He knocked three times, as usual. His favorite number.

"Three knocks. Has to be Chase," Mrs. Stevens said.

Tripp's dad opened the door, and Chase burst into the room, his hair mussed and his orange shirt untucked. He looked a little crazy. Daisy was with him, wagging her tail. Even she looked excited.

Chase was surprised to see Tripp's dad open the door. Daisy didn't look as surprised.

"Come on and sit down with us," Tripp's mom said.

"Thanks, but I already ate," Chase replied.

"Okay, but you can sit with us. I want to say grace. I'm happy we're all eating together tonight. But she can sit over there." She pointed Daisy to the living room, where the dog curled up and promptly fell asleep. She'd been to the Stevens' house enough to know there wouldn't be any food for her.

"When did you get home?" Chase asked Mr. Stevens. He wore shorts and a T-shirt, but these were clean and obviously not what he would have worn all day at the Destroyers' practice in the intense Florida heat.

"About an hour ago," Mr. Stevens said. "After being in California for the last couple of days, I told them that I was cutting out early to see all you guys." He'd been scouting players at various colleges that the

Destroyers might consider for selection in next year's player draft.

As a pro scout for the team, Tripp's dad had three totally different parts to his job: sitting in his dark office watching video of football games; standing outside at practice watching the Destroyers go through practice; and flying to colleges all around the country—where he also sat in dark offices and stood out at practice watching various teams and players go through their paces.

"Well, I'm up! Almost!"

Tripp grinned.

"Up?" Kayla asked. She was tiny, just in sixth grade, with freckles and braces.

"Up on varsity!" He and Tripp high-fived.

"I didn't tell them," Tripp said proudly. "I kept your secret."

"Is it for this week?" Tripp's dad asked. He high-fived Chase too.

"Don't know yet. And who knows? Maybe it won't happen at all, but Coach Skalaski said he might need me soon."

"You're a really good player," Mr. Stevens said. "But I'm surprised with JB at quarterback that they already need you to move up."

"Well, he didn't exactly say that they *need* me, at least not at quarterback. I'm guessing it might be Senior Skip Day. I think they just need somebody or something with a pulse ... who, of course, can look great in a uniform," Chase said, and they all laughed.

After dinner was over, Mr. Stevens walked toward his office. Chase followed him. "Hey, Chase. What's up?"

"I hate to bother you again tonight, but—"

"It's never a bother," said Tripp's dad.

"Thanks, I always like hearing that." Chase looked serious.

Chase was a lot quieter than he'd been only an hour ago, when he bounced into the house, filled with excitement. Thinking of his dad sometimes made him sad. Other times, he felt a little nervous too, especially when talking to Mr. Stevens about him, since Mr. Stevens felt like a real dad to Chase. Chase continued to speak. "Well, my dad called the other day just to catch up and see how we were doing—" Mr. Stevens nodded. "—and he has a client in Detroit and he was hoping to take him to the Destroyers game when you guys play Detroit up at their stadium next month, and, well ... but if it's a problem, you know, then ..."

Mr. Stevens jumped in to save Chase from his discomfort. "Oh, I guess the game is sold out and your dad couldn't get tickets. Well, let me check on my end to see if I can buy tickets for him."

"No, Sir, I don't think it is sold out. He can buy tickets by calling Detroit if he has to, he said, but he just wondered if you could get better tickets than he could get, it would be good for his client and stuff."

"Let me do some checking and I'll get back with you. One last thing, Chase. I forgot to mention it with your exciting news earlier, but tomorrow I'm calling your mom to figure out dates to get to a pro game road trip — all three of us."

Chase cheered up again at the mention of a game, and hung out for a few minutes longer, then bounded out of the house with Daisy at his side.

"See you tomorrow!" Tripp called as Chase headed across the darkened lawn.

CHAPTER 5

Chase walked out to practice on Wednesday afternoon to find a buzz in the air.

"What's going on?" he asked.

Nick Wood answered. "Coach Skalaski called us over to their field as soon as we're done stretching!" Chase groaned to himself. A varsity/junior varsity scrimmage. Most of the guys were excited, but Chase hadn't played much in the earlier scrimmage. Because there were two senior quarterbacks, Coach Skalaski had let them both play, while Chase only got a few plays for the JV.

He ran over with the rest of the JV guys after stretching. He tried not to envy the players who had made the varsity after summer tryouts, but it was hard not to. Their practice jerseys were nicer than the JV game jerseys, with their sharp teal and green. Coach Skalaski, the varsity head coach, gathered the boys around him.

"Same rules as before. JV vs. varsity, but we'll switch a couple of guys around from JV to varsity. And *no tackling*! Let 'em run! Other teams will be trying to knock our guys out of games, we're not going to do it to each other!" Everyone nodded. Chase had seen it before. The defense was only supposed to tag the player with the ball, the way they would in two-hand touch football, but let him keep running toward the end zone. The coaches would put the ball down for the next play where he'd been tagged, but Coach Skalaski liked the ball carrier to get used to running toward the end zone, even after contact. A lot of teams do that, even in the pros, or so Mr. Stevens had told Chase and Tripp before.

Coach Skalaski walked over to Chase and handed him a red jersey, the universal symbol for *I'm a quarterback, don't tackle me*. Number eleven. He was normally number three, but in scrimmages he'd take whatever temporary jersey they gave him.

"I've got you quarterbacking the JV and Roger in charge of the varsity. We'll let JB sit this one out — it's a long season." Chase was thrilled but tried to be cool and not smile.

In the last scrimmage Roger quarterbacked the JV and JB the varsity squad, so that both varsity quarterbacks could get practice. Chase put on the red *don't tackle me* jersey and headed over to the sideline. The varsity took the ball first, and Roger led them down the field for a touchdown. Coach Skalaski brought the ball back out to the 8-yard line and had the varsity work on "red zone" plays — plays inside the 20-yard line, close to the other team's end zone.

Finally, Coach put the ball down on the JV's own 20-yard line and let them take over.

Chase called the cadence — "*Blue 17, Blue 17, Hut, Hut!*" — and handed off to Robbie for a gain of three yards before Robbie was touched. Next was a pass play to Drew. It hit him right in the hands, but Drew dropped it! Chase tried not to be upset, but some of his teammates just weren't very good.

Coach Preston encouraged them both. "Good throw, Chase! Drew, keep your eyes on it! Catch it with your hands ... don't let it hit your chest!" Chase sighed and got back in the huddle.

Then Chase tried another pass play to Mark. Chase called the cadence. "*Blue 17, Blue 17, Hut, Hut!*" He took the snap from Solomon and dropped three steps back and started to throw when he felt a big hand slap him on the chest. As he fell he threw the ball. Incomplete!

"Back on the ball! Back on the ball!" Chase heard Coach Skalaski's voice call out. "Let's replay third down."

"But he was sacked before he threw it," someone grumbled. "Jerome touched him before he threw it."

"We're replaying third down because Jerome hit him too hard," Coach Skalaski said. "No hitting the quarterbacks! Everybody knows that. Get on the ball, run the same play."

Chase had seen Coach Skalaski do that before, give the JV an advantage if they weren't doing well, which was quite often, since the varsity was so much bigger. Chase ran the play, but since it was the same play, it had no chance of succeeding — the varsity guys knew that it was coming and knocked the pass down.

Coach Skalaski put the ball back on the 20-yard line line and turned the two teams around. "Riverside!" he yelled, the term to switch sides of the ball.

Now the varsity had to go eighty yards for a touchdown.

Chase trotted toward the sideline and passed Roger coming onto the field. "Nice throw, Squirt," Roger hissed as he passed. Chase stopped and looked back as Roger passed, but the senior quarterback had his back to him. Moments later, Roger was in the huddle.

What was that about?

On the next play, Roger found Tripp with a perfect spiral and varsity did go the distance for the TD. Chase marveled as Tripp's number eighty-two caught the ball in stride and streaked down the sideline, running it in for an 80-yard score. Tripp was big and fast, especially for an eighth-grader. Chase was thrilled for him. He was also disappointed that his scrimmage was going so poorly — and that he was still on the JV.

Roger ran past him and smirked.

They ran a few more plays before Coach Skalaski sent them back to their own field to finish practice with Coach Preston. All in all, not a great day. But JV/varsity scrimmages often didn't go very well. At least, not for Chase and the JV.

Chase raced to the locker room. He needed to get home — dinner plans, for once. He saw Tripp coming off the varsity field as he was heading toward his bike. "See ya, Thug!" he yelled.

Tripp flipped his hair from his eyes. "See ya, Thug!" he yelled back.

Chase raced home and then he and Hannah went to the Browns' house for dinner. They'd been invited by Megan, and Chase was thrilled with the thought of being at JB's, especially after such a lousy scrimmage.

Once they arrived, he was pretty nervous and stood off to the side while Mrs. Brown's voice echoed through the house, calling the family to dinner. Moments later Chase heard the faint sound of the music of Lecrae's "Tell the World" from upstairs come to a stop, and JB's voice drifted down the stairs.

"Be right there!" he called.

JB's sister, Megan, had arrived at the table, joining Chase and Hannah, who watched as Megan's little brother, Scotty, came into the kitchen from the garage.

"Chase, would you go get JB, please?" Mrs. Brown said. Chase stood but hesitated. "It's the second door on the left up the stairs," she said, and Chase headed up.

JB was at his desk, closing the ESPN window on his computer browser. "Chase. I didn't realize you were here," JB said, smiling his broad, usual smile.

"Megan invited us," Chase said. He was so excited to be there. It was turning into a great week—maybe getting called up to varsity, now dinner at the Browns.

"Glad you're here," JB said. The way he said it, Chase really believed him.

"So, looking at sports?" Chase asked. It sounded kind of stupid, but he was nervous.

"Oh, that." JB stood and closed the laptop. "Just checking out who the Heat play tonight."

"You like the Heat? I do," said Chase. Again, it sounded stupid coming out of his mouth.

JB motioned him toward the door and nodded. "Come on, let's go downstairs. My mom's ready, right?" Chase nodded, wishing he could've thought of something else—anything else—to say.

They headed down the hall, and JB spoke again. "Hey, I wanted to talk to you about your cadence."

"Sure," Chase said. *What?*

"I watched you today. You looked good, although your little guys were having trouble blocking the varsity guys. Or catching your passes, too. But I wanted to ask—do you always say, 'Blue 17, Blue 17'?"

Chase shook his head yes and JB smiled. "That's fine, but you probably ought to change it up every now and then."

53

"I didn't think it mattered, as long as I don't use the live colors."

"It doesn't matter — to *your* team. But it will matter to the defense. What are your live colors right now?"

"Red for run, green for pass," Chase answered. "And our two runs are 41 and 42." JB nodded.

They were standard plays. The tailback — the "4" — would get the handoff and carry the ball through either the "1" hole, to the left of the center, or the "2" hole, to the right of the center. Hence 41 or 42. Tailback left or Tailback right.

"Plus, we've got a couple of passes that go with green."

The "live" color was the quarterback's signal to his teammates that he was changing the play at the line of scrimmage — an audible. If he didn't use a live color, but instead used anything else, like blue, orange, yellow, gold, white, black, pink, or turquoise, then the players knew that they were going to run whatever play was called in the huddle. If, however, Chase called, "Red 42," for instance, they knew to disregard the play from the huddle and they would go with a running play — the tailback through the two hole.

"The problem," JB said, "comes when you say 'Blue 17' almost every play. Once the defense hears another color like red or green, they'll know that you're up to something. That's why I switch it up. I'll call 'White 42' or 'Black 41' or 'Blue 33,' on pass plays — and none of those names mean anything. But the defense can't tell that. So when I finally do mix in 'Red 41,' they don't realize that I'm switching to a run." Chase agreed. That made sense.

"You've just got to stay alert and make sure you stay away from red or green — unless you mean it."

Chase grinned. "Thanks. That's helpful."

Everyone gathered at the table, and Dr. Brown thanked Hannah and Chase for coming to dinner.

"Yes, the pleasure is ours," added Scotty, and everyone laughed. Megan had filled Chase in on Scotty while their mom was driving them over to the Brown house. Scotty was eight years old and had a crazy sense of humor, always saying funny things. He was a handful for an eight-year-old.

"This is Hannah," Megan said.

"Oh yes. You've had her over here a lot," JB said.

Chase had never been to their house. He'd been surprised when he got home from practice Monday and Hannah said that the Browns had invited him too. He tried to think of something to say to JB. "So, do you like Lecrae?"

"I do," said JB. "And Chris Tomlin and others too."

"Cool." Chase knew Lecrae. A little.

The group settled down, said the blessing, and started passing food around the table.

Megan spoke up. "You all have met Dad before, right?" Chase and Hannah nodded as their dad spoke up, wearing a green William & Mary T-shirt. "Feel free to call me Mr. Brown. Everyone does."

Megan's black leggings and loose, baggy, bright pink top were a stark contrast from her skin, the color of dark chocolate. Her legs seemed twice as long as his, Chase thought. Although she could have passed for a model, with her striking good looks, she couldn't help but be annoyed when people assumed she was a cheerleader and not a player.

JB was the oldest of the three Brown children by four years, a senior at Carr High and not only the starting quarterback on the football team, but also the shooting guard on the varsity basketball team. Megan told Hannah that as long as he stayed focused, JB would probably end up being the valedictorian of the senior class as well. He might be the most popular guy in the school too, and Chase couldn't quite believe he was at his house.

JB was wearing a gray sweater vest over a light blue short sleeve shirt and a pair of dark, stone-washed jeans. He looked like a magazine model for one of those cool, hip magazines. He wore vests almost year-round, Chase had noticed. He must *never* get cold, he thought. JB's muscled arms were always bare, until it just got too hot in the summers and he ditched the vests. Vests were a thing for JB.

Chase would probably wear them too, if he had biceps like that. During dinner, JB's mom called him "farmer strong."

"What's that?" Hannah asked.

"He gets most of his strength naturally, from working around the house and in the yard. Plus, he used to help on a friend's farm when he was a small boy, splitting trees."

"Splitting trees?" Chase asked.

"That's not half as bad as watching him chase calves!" Scotty called out.

The Browns all started laughing, as JB tried to protest that it wasn't that funny.

"Oh, honey, it was so funny," Mrs. Brown said.

"Wonderful. Just wonderful," Dr. Brown added.

"He was slipping and falling in the muddy field — it had just rained — trying to catch this one calf. He never did get it."

"But he got plenty of mud," Dr. Brown chimed.

Chase knew JB was seventeen but thought he looked older, especially sitting right there. He was about the size of Mr. Stevens, who had played pro football. Chase guessed he was already 6 foot 3 inches tall, and just under 200 pounds. He knew JB was large and solid. His shoulders were wide, and his hands large enough to easily grip a football or basketball. Chase figured the wet-ball drills weren't a problem for JB the way they were for him.

"How was school today, y'all?" Dr. Brown asked. Chase hadn't been around the family much, and had certainly never been to dinner before. But Hannah told him that he was a medical doctor. He was doing research at the University of Florida into what makes people twitch, she'd said. He was involved in really complicated brain surgeries. But he still wanted to be called "Mister."

Scotty piped up to answer the question. "It was a good day. I think I'm getting the hang of this reading thing. Plus, I didn't get sent to the office one time."

JB and Megan grinned while they rolled their eyes at their brother's jokes, and their parents laughed. Hannah had told Chase that Scotty had been reading and doing multiplication since he was three.

"What happened to your shirt?" Dr. Brown asked. Scotty's yellow Oregon Ducks T-shirt was dirty and torn.

"No big thing. But you should see the *other* guy," he said. His face was totally serious. And then he laughed.

JB looked over at Scotty. Chase liked the way JB looked at his brother and smiled. Warmly. Kind, maybe even proud. In fact, come to think about it, JB seemed to look at everyone like that. Chase realized that you just felt better when JB looked at you and smiled.

"I was playing outside behind Luke's house today," Scotty finally said.

"You're going to need a shower," Dr. Brown told him. Scotty nodded.

The Browns were easy to talk to, which was a good thing, since Hannah and Megan were talking with each other the whole meal.

After dinner, Dr. Brown announced it was time for their daily devotional.

Chase looked at Hannah, and she just shrugged. JB noticed, and said, "We try to do this most every night. Eat together and have a little devotional."

Dr. Brown kept it short, reading from the Bible about the fruit of the Spirit: " ... love, joy, peace, forbearance, kindness, goodness, faithfulness, gentleness and self-control."

Megan piped up. "I'm doing great at self-control!" Everyone chuckled, but Hannah started laughing — loud.

"Oh no. Now what?" asked Mrs. Brown.

"Well, I asked some kids at lunch if they were going to the game Friday, and – "

"Wait! Let me guess," Scotty said. JB was nodding too. Chase figured they knew what was coming. "And somebody thought you were a cheerleader!"

"And you got mad!" jumped in JB. Everyone was laughing while Megan looked sheepish.

"You really have to control your tongue, young lady," said Dr. Brown. "That's the main thing for you to grasp." He looked at Chase and Hannah. "Actually, that's a hard one for all of us to learn — patience," he said.

Chase kind of liked the devotional. Even though his mom took them to church, he wasn't sure he'd heard people talking about God anywhere else — and certainly not laughing while they were doing it! Plus, it was nice and short. He was itching to get home and go over his oral report due the next day. He rubbed the notecards in his back pocket. He needed to practice again.

Moments later they all got up from the table and Megan asked JB for a ride.

"Where you going?" he asked.

"To Hannah's," she replied. "They need a ride home, and I'm going to stay there and study for a while with her." JB nodded.

"I'll go grab my keys."

"Already did. I'll be at your car," Megan said, handing the keys to JB.

The drive only took about five minutes, as he headed east down County Road 229, south past Carr High, and then a mile back out west on Nelson Street. He turned his old silver Honda Accord down the long driveway to the Clarks' house.

"Wow. Not many neighbors." In fact, Tripp's was the only other house in sight. About fifty yards behind the two houses was a forest of pine trees and fairly thick underbrush. It was too dark to see the treehouse that Chase and Tripp had built in the woods a couple of years before.

"Hmm. If that forest wasn't so dense, I think it'd be quicker for you to walk out the back of their house and back home when you're done tonight," JB said.

Megan rolled her eyes. She knew that their parents wouldn't allow her to walk home by herself after dark.

And she knew that JB knew that his parents would kill him if he let her do that. Of course, Megan knew that JB would never let her walk home after dark, either.

"I'll call you when I'm done. Actually, don't worry about it. Maybe I will walk home." She smiled mischievously.

JB answered immediately. "No you wo–" and saw her trying to keep a straight face. "Aren't you funny?" He looked over at the other house. "Did you say Tripp lives over there?" JB pointed toward it, as Megan and the others climbed out of the car.

"Yeah." Megan hopped out.

CHAPTER 6

The following afternoon after lunch, Chase had to present his American history report. It had been a good day so far, but he was worried about what his voice might do. He'd spent lunch in the library so he could read over the notes for his report.

They were giving reports on people of the twentieth century. Some of the kids had spoken about Neil Armstrong, Colin Powell, Tony Dungy. Chase picked Archie Carr, the school's namesake.

Coach Preston sat at his teacher desk in teacher mode. Daniel, who was a total certified techno-genius, finished giving his talk on Steve Jobs, one of the founders of Apple Computer.

Chase was up next. He cleared his throat. Prayed that God would keep his voice strong.

"Around 1970," he began, "sea turtles were dying

off. Fast. So Dr. Carr started tracking them, trying to figure out if people were killing them or if something else was happening."

Tripp raised his hand, and Coach Preston told him to wait for Chase to finish.

Chase looked at his note cards. He'd been talking faster than he'd been turning them. He lost his train of thought and flipped through them frantically. He could feel the sweat gathering on his forehead.

There! Finally, he found where he'd been.

"Oil spills and other types of water pollution affect the sea turtles' health and habitat. Thanks to Dr. Carr's discoveries, more efforts were made to help. Over time, sea turtles have gotten better and stopped dying as quickly."

Chase looked up for the briefest of moments. *Big mistake!* He caught Tripp's eye, and he couldn't help himself. He just started laughing. Chase couldn't help but glance back at Tripp again, who now had his head on his desk. Tripp's shoulders were shaking with silent laughter.

Just finish and get it over with, Chase thought. He saw Coach Preston shaking his head, but at least he was smiling.

"Okay, " Chase said. "So after Carr died, the United States dedicated a National Wildlife Refuge on the East Coast of Florida and named it after him. It's a big patch of dark beach where turtles can come lay their eggs and people won't step on their nests. Back then, this school used to be called River County, and we were the Rivermen."

"Rivermen, ha!" someone hollered from the back of the room.

"Did we even have a rowing team back then?" Mark asked, earning a couple of groans.

"Is Loggerheads any better than Rivermen?" Megan inquired.

"Good point," Nick said.

"Enough!" Coach Preston exclaimed, motioning for quiet.

"The way we became Carr is because of the principal back then," Chase checked his cards, "Principal McGuyver. He let the students decide on a new mascot. There were four mascots they could choose between: Loggerheads, River Dogs, Gators, and Banana Spiders."

"Banana spiders!" Mark said.

"I know, right?" Chase said.

"Banana spiders are indigenous to Florida," Coach Preston said. "That is, they are found here."

Chase looked back at his notes. "Some people believed Gators had really won the vote. But Principal McGuyver had gone to Florida State, whose rival was the University of Florida Gators, and McGuyver was against that idea. Anyway, whether that rumor is true or not, he announced the winner of the vote was Loggerheads, and the school board then decided to rename the school in honor of Archie F. Carr."

He made it to the end of his report. *Phew*! But he noticed Kate was engaged in his report, and so he kept talking. He changed his voice, like he was hosting an episode of *Unsolved Mysteries*. "Principal McGuyver denied that he stuffed the ballot box and said it was only sour grapes by Gators fans. But then ... he mysteriously disappeared, never to be heard from again!"

"Dun-dun-dun-duunnnnnn ..." Tripp piled on the sound effects.

"Mr. McGuyver's whereabouts are unknown to this day, but according to Wikipedia, there have been several alleged sightings by the North Florida UFO Society, River County Chapter."

Coach Preston stood and clapped. "Excellent! Well done, Chase! Good facts, fun story. Tripp, did you have a question? You had your hand raised."

"I forget," said Tripp. He shrugged.

The class laughed.

Coach Preston always made Tripp wait, and Tripp seemed to forget his question most of the time.

Coach checked his watch. "Okay, we're about a minute early. You may go, but stay quiet in the halls. Chase, you and Nick stick around for a minute, please."

Nick Wood played both receiver and running back on the JV football team with Chase, and Coach Preston went up to the whiteboard with them.

He wanted to put in a new play, *Rex Gun 300 Octane*, that he thought they would need that night. "Newberry is a big school. They've also got a big, physical, and good team. We need a new play to throw at them."

Everyone knew that Coach Skalaski not only scheduled games for his varsity team but also oversaw the entire football operation at Carr. Often and intentionally, Coach scheduled those larger, more physical opponents for the JV team in an effort to push and develop those players. His theory was that by forcing the kids at 4A Carr High School, with just under 900 kids in the entire school, to play schools in higher classifications, it would help them develop into better players in the future for the Carr varsity. Lincoln was a small town, but the people were proud of Carr football, which was improving every year. "Their kids may be bigger, but ours are smarter and more disciplined," Tripp told Chase that Coach Skalaski would tell the varsity at practice frequently.

Suddenly, the class bell went off as Coach was diagramming the play. "Okay, you're late."

"Before we go, one question — should we even run that play?" Chase asked. "I mean, the way the receiver is lined up ... he might get completely clocked on a tackle after catching the pass. Wouldn't it be dangerous to him?"

Coach Preston shook his head. "Not if the quarterback throws the ball early, before the defense has a chance to react. Then he should be fine." Typical coach answer, thought Chase. *The quarterback's responsibility to make everything work. And keep everyone safe.*

He took them to his desk and wrote a note. "Now hurry up and get to your next class!"

As they walked down the hall, Chase asked, "What did you think?"

"About what?" Nick wondered.

"Didn't that seem weird, keeping us after class to put in a new play? I mean, he made us late —"

"Plus, we never add plays. You're right — it does seem a little different, trying to put in a new play, especially on the day of the game."

"Yeah, we haven't done that all year," Chase added.

They arrived at their lockers and split up.

"See you this afternoon," Nick called out as he disappeared.

By the time school was over, Chase still hadn't heard anything about being called up to the varsity team. He stuck with the JV and got ready for the game, playing the Newberry Panthers.

They *were* really big. Much bigger than Carr. The Carr JV always seemed outnumbered, and the players were usually smaller, too, than their opponents. Even the varsity seemed shorthanded on Friday nights, which was part of how Tripp made the varsity. The varsity played ten games while the JV only played seven. Another reason the varsity needed more players.

Chase and Carr High played well and he was thankful that the skies were clear and there was no rain. It was hot, though. Way too hot for the middle of

October. By the end of the first quarter they were only losing by a score of 7 – 6, and by halftime, the score was tied at 14 – 14 after they scored a touchdown and got the two-point conversion. They hadn't made one extra point kick all year on JV.

Chase often complained to Megan that she should be the JV kicker. "You're only in eighth grade. You should be helping *us*, not varsity." She always laughed at his jokes. But he really did wish they had another kicker — Drew was a decent receiver but a terrible kicker.

"You won't be saying that when you're on the varsity too," she'd reply with a laugh. He knew she was right. Coach Preston had wanted Chase to call the new play, *Rex Gun 300 Octane*, twice so far in the game and both times players had messed it up by jumping across the line of scrimmage too early. Chase hoped Coach wouldn't ask Chase to call it again. The players just didn't know the play.

Late in the fourth quarter, the Loggerheads had fallen behind but they were trying to finish off a frantic comeback to win the game. Chase threw a short pass to Mark who turned and ran the ball forty yards down the field for a touchdown!

There were two minutes left in the game and the Loggerheads had to try an on-side kick to have a chance. They kicked it, the ball took a high bounce, and Mark recovered it! The Loggerheads had one final chance to score!

With no receivers open on first down, Chase tucked the ball and ran out of bounds after a 10-yard gain. Several plays later, Chase could *feel* it. They were so close to coming back to win.

This time, it would happen. Everything was going their way.

Coach Preston nodded to Chase for *Rex Gun 300 Octane*. Again. Chase threw the pass deep down the field but he never saw the safety. Carson, the receiver on the right side of the play, ran the wrong direction, and brought his defender with him to the area that Chase threw. His pass sailed deep in the end zone to his wide receiver on the left, Drew, and was intercepted by the Newberry free safety. Carson had brought him right to the ball.

Again, not knowing the play *Rex Gun 300 Octane* had hurt them.

Game over. But at least the new play hadn't gotten the receiver hurt.

Tripp sat with the Clarks at the game and rode home with them. They'd waited at the school until Chase returned on the team with the bus, and now Tripp and Chase stood in the driveway in the cool, night air. There weren't many streetlights in their area and the stars were bright tonight in Lincoln.

"You were awesome tonight, Chase. Again."

"Yeah, but we lost. Again." Chase was quiet. He despised losing. Tripp tried to cheer him up.

"You know it doesn't matter. And even if it did, you're still playing well. Just wait 'til JB and Roger graduate — this year — and you keep getting better. You've got a strong arm for such a little, scrawny guy ..."

"Hey!" Chase clenched his fists, acting like he was upset. They hadn't ever been in a fight, which was probably a good thing for Chase. Tripp had hit a growth spurt and had gained pounds and inches over the last summer.

"You coming to our game tomorrow?" Tripp asked.

"I don't think so. It's kind of a long drive to North Sumter. I doubt my mom will want to go after a full week of lawyer stuff."

"You'll have to come next week. We're playing Jacksonville Raines. They're like number three in the state. Oh — maybe you'll be playing with us by then, anyway!" Tripp paused and acted like he was thinking. "Actually, nevermind. I shouldn't have said anything."

"What?" Chase asked. He was worried.

"Well, you know, you're probably too scrawny for varsity ..." Tripp took off and Chase realized the joke and was in hot pursuit, running across the grass toward Tripp's house. Chase finally slowed and yelled, "I'll get you, when you least expect it!"

Tripp laughed, and disappeared through the garage door with a call of "See ya, Thug!" It wasn't like the old days, when they were on the same team, but it felt good, spending time together again.

CHAPTER 7

Monday, Chase headed out to the JV practice as usual. Tripp and the varsity team had beaten North Sumter 24 – 13. Tripp caught three passes and Megan kicked a long field goal, but Chase hadn't gone. It was too far away, and his mother was tired. That was fine by Chase. He hadn't really felt like watching the other guys playing varsity, anyway.

JB had another huge game passing and running the football, and there were rumors around school that coaches from the University of Florida and Miami would be at this week's upcoming game to watch him. He already had a scholarship offer from Florida State and from what Chase gathered, every other college he'd every heard of.

On Chase's way to the field, Coach Skalaski pulled him aside.

"When you're all done out there with your practice today," he said, "I want you to come over to our field and start to get familiar with how we do things while we're together."

Chase gulped and nodded. "Yes, sir."

It was a grueling practice, with steam rising out of the grass as the Florida heat baked the players and field. Other guys kept getting water, but Chase never noticed. He just wanted practice over so he could join the varsity team.

Finally it was, and with JV practice behind him, he trotted over to the varsity field. Varsity! With their longer practices, fancier practice uniforms, and bigger bodies. Much bigger bodies.

Several others from JV were headed in that direction as well. Apparently coach had talked to a few players, including Solomon Williams and Nick Wood about getting familiar with varsity. They stood together, off to the side of the field.

"Where should we go?" Solomon whispered to Chase.

"I don't have any idea. Let's just stand here," responded Chase. Solomon nodded. After a few moments, Coach gathered the entire team together and called Chase and the others over by waving his hand in their direction.

"Gentlemen," he began, "you know that I'm a big fan of Chuck Noll." Chuck Noll had won four Super Bowls as the head coach of the Pittsburgh Steelers, Coach's favorite team, and was his favorite coach. "Coach Noll always preached that champions become champions not by doing anything extraordinary, but rather simply by doing ordinary things better than anyone else. Other people *could* do those ordinary things, but choose not to."

Chase was glued to Coach's words. Others, however, were restless, but Chase didn't notice. The players all around him. The jerseys. He was locked into everything being said. He had waited for this moment for so long!

Coach took a drink from his water bottle and continued. "Coach Noll once said, 'Leaving the game plan is a sign of panic, and panic is not in our game plan.' Well, I'm telling you all right now that *skipping school* is not in our game plan either! I understand Senior Skip Day is next week, and skipping will not be tolerated here."

Chase and Tripp exchanged glances. Chase had forgotten about Skip Day. He was an eighth-grader, after all. "While some of you might be considering skipping, know that there will be consequences, so choose carefully."

There was shuffling and muttering from the guys. "Come on, Coach," Roger said. "It's a tradition."

Bad idea, Chase thought.

Coach's eyes were bulging. "You have the *privilege* of wearing this uniform. Therefore, you are role models. You are expected to live up to a certain standard."

Chase looked at JB and wondered if he was planning

to skip. If so, he hid it well. JB's face remained passive, his eyes on the coach.

"Starters or not, you skip, there will be consequences," Coach continued.

As the team left the field, Coach gathered Chase and the few other JV players around him. "I don't want you to worry about Friday. Just want to put you at ease." Chase's heart started thumping. Who would have to miss the game? Chase, maybe playing quarterback for the varsity and only in eighth grade!

Coach continued, "We want you to play in the last JV game this week, but you'll practice with us during the week. And we want you to dress with us on Friday. You won't be able to play but we might need you as backup for the playoffs."

Chase and Solomon understood that per league rules, they couldn't play in a JV *and* varsity game in the same week. Still, they were psyched to be able to dress with the team!

They all nodded, vigorously and simultaneously.

"Let's see how it goes. I want you to show me what you've got during practice! And depending how things turn out in the playoff picture … well, let's not get ahead of ourselves here. This will be a lot of work, okay?"

"Okay!" Chase said eagerly. *I'm so ready for this!* Staying on varsity, any way they wanted him to and especially with playoffs looming, sounded awesome.

"Once it's time to play, for you defensive guys, our

defense is just the same as yours. Those of you on offense," — Chase looked over at Nick and Solomon, the only other offensive players — "don't need to worry about learning our offense. We will probably have to use you on special teams, covering kickoffs or punts, but we won't make you play offense. That would be too much in just a couple of days. Although, it's just the same stuff — and the game might speed up some with older guys around you." Coach turned toward Chase. "If JB can't play, we'll go with Roger. If it's an emergency, we'll put Tripp back there. Although he's not a quarterback, he knows the plays. We can have him just run the ball. I don't want you to worry."

Chase tried to hide his disappointment. He was anything but worried. He'd been thrilled at the thought of being put in at quarterback. Now he was still excited at being on the varsity, but his hopes for quick fame were apparently dashed.

After practice, the excitement was back and Chase ran across the wide lawn to Tripp's house. After Coach had talked to the JV guys, Chase hadn't seen Tripp again. He headed by his own house to grab Daisy, then they headed across the yard to the Stevens' house.

Dusk was settling in as he arrived. Chase knocked his usual three times and ran in with Daisy when Kayla opened the door. Daisy usually barked at most anyone who moved — at either house — but not at the Stevens family. Even though they didn't feed her people food.

Chase ran in and saw Tripp. "I missed you after practice! Tried to find you!"

"Yeah, I figured I'd better get home and get started on homework."

Kayla and Tripp's mom were there too, and Chase was surprised again to see Tripp's father in the family room as well. Chase couldn't remember running into Tripp's dad so much for dinner during football season, because of traveling so much for the Destroyers.

"Hey, Chase," said Tripp's dad, and the others greeted him as well.

Chase looked puzzled, and said to Mr. Stevens, "Why are you here?"

Tripp's father smiled. "Seems like you ask me that a lot lately." He smiled. "I had been on the road scouting this week," he answered. "They sent me to look at a couple of colleges in Ohio and Indiana, and I just flew back into town. That's where the cold weather is! Man, it was freezing!"

The concept of *freezing* was hard to believe, since it was so hot they still didn't have to wear a jacket in Lincoln. It was hard to imagine cooling off anytime soon. "Anyway, since I've been gone for three days, I landed and drove straight here. I didn't even bother to go down to the stadium. The views are better here." Mr. Stevens' office was deep inside the stadium, along with the other Destroyers offices, with no windows. His running joke as long as Chase had known him was "my beautiful wife and daughter are a much better view" than his view at work in his windowless office.

The boys couldn't disagree. Mrs. Stevens was very pretty and Kayla was really cute, with her braces. When she wasn't being an irritating little sister.

Chase thought Mr. Stevens had the world's greatest job, but Mr. Stevens always told him that it wasn't that much fun, especially if you were a football fan.

"No," Mr. Stevens said, "it is not a great job for a true fan like you. We'll go to a game and you'll see for yourself."

That night, Chase and the Stevens family talked about nothing other than his promotion to the varsity. "Yep," Tripp said, "one of these days it'll be Clark-to-Stevens for a big completion." Tripp was a really good player and was big for his age, like his dad had been. Mr. Stevens played two years in professional football for the Oakland Marauders after a college career at Brown University.

"I hope so," said Chase. "I'm just excited to be up with you guys."

Tripp's mood turned serious. "I still think the seniors are going to skip tomorrow," he said.

"You're kidding!" said Tripp's mom. "After all that Coach said? Tripp was just telling us about Coach's warning when you got here."

"Yeah, they were all talking after practice that it was something that they felt like they had to do as part of the senior class." Tripp shook his mop of blond hair and shrugged his shoulders. Chase, although of decent build for middle school, felt dwarfed by the taller Tripp.

Mr. Stevens sighed. "They need to learn some responsibility."

As for Chase, he didn't really care if they learned or not. In fact, he kind of hoped they didn't learn just yet. All he could think about right then was that he was headed to varsity. He told Mr. Stevens that Coach said Tripp might play quarterback in an emergency.

"Ugh. That sounds terrible," said Tripp.

"What? I mean, *good*. That sounds really *good*." Tripp laughed as Chase spoke. "Why would it be terrible?"

"I'd rather just stay where I am. After almost two months, I finally know what to do and where to be. Pretty much, anyway. I'm finally getting it all figured out. That'd be confusing."

Mr. Stevens nodded. "Plus, as quarterback, you have to know what *everyone* does. It's easier to just keep track of your own job — like Tripp does at receiver."

"Good. Tripp, tell Coach you want *me* to play."

Tripp chuckled. "Definitely."

Mr. Stevens spoke up. "Guys, your primary job is to do what you're told. Whatever you're told. Don't say anything to Coach, Tripp. Hopefully everyone does what they're supposed to and nothing happens."

Chase looked disappointed but understood. He checked his watch — time to head home.

"See ya, Thug."

"Yeah, see ya, Thug." Mr. and Mrs. Stevens shook their heads and rolled their eyes. Tripp and Chase were good kids and good students — as far from "thugs" as possible.

CHAPTER 8

The next morning was a beautiful one, and it seemed like a perfect day to Chase. Even as Chase left Daisy and jumped on his bike alongside Tripp, headed for school, the sun was low but bright, and the sky was clear, a washed out, faded blue Florida sky.

"Hope I get called up," he said under his breath, but Tripp couldn't hear him as they pedaled off to school. He liked the sound of it.

He hadn't been back over to the Browns, although Megan was still coming by his house plenty. He kept looking for her in the halls, hoping to find out if JB had skipped school that day. He saw her once, from a distance, but had to get to class so he didn't have time to talk. The halls seemed emptier, as if students were absent, but he couldn't tell who.

Chase dressed out and took the field that afternoon

well before he needed to. He passed the time catching kickoffs from Megan, who was warming up before practice. She was out at practice even before he was, so he couldn't ask then. He thought he'd wait until she was done and ask about JB before practice officially started, but as soon as she finished, Coach Skalaski called everyone up.

Chase knelt with the rest of the team looped around Coach in a large circle. Every guy was there. Maybe no one went to the beach for Senior Skip Day. Chase felt a little disappointed.

Coach Skalaski spoke, his voice quiet, with strain evident in every word. "I am extremely disappointed in you seniors who participated in Senior Skip Day today. While I appreciate you cutting short your beach time to return to practice, I know who you are because the front office gave me a list." He then proceeded to read off names. *A lot of names*, Chase thought. *But no JB.* Chase glanced over at JB, who was grinning at him again.

Weird. JB always seemed to be grinning at him.

"Those players may take off their shoulder pads for the day." There were groans. Coach's voice rose quickly and lost its strain. He sounded mad now, not upset. "I don't want to hear one word from you guys! You have a responsibility to your teammates, and so far you have failed to live up to that." Coach went from excited to yelling, and the veins in his neck were like cords, strained tight against his skin. "You may spend the *rest* of this practice running, I haven't decided! Start now! Get out of my sight!"

It was the beginning of practice, so Chase thought that sounded awful. The rains that had been coming down all fall finally stopped this week, but it still felt like summer. The temperatures were still in the 90s in the afternoons. Tripp caught his eye and made a face. It was really hot to be running, but seven seniors started to jog off around the outside edge of the practice field.

"Keep running around the field until I blow my whistle," Coach yelled. "At which point you may get water. Until then, keep running!" He turned to Coach Quinn, and spoke calmly. "You be in charge of the whistle and water, please, Coach. Plenty of breaks."

He then turned back to the rest of the team. "Gentlemen, we've got our work cut out for us. For you young guys, here's how this is going to work. During practice, we run—between drills, during drills. Everywhere. Do not walk. Do not put your helmet down. Either have it in your hand or have it on your head. And if it's on your head, then strap it on."

They broke into units, offense running to one end of the field, while the defense stayed in the middle. Chase glanced quickly over at the JV practice and Coach Preston, far off, it seemed, on the other field. He then turned his attention back to varsity practice. The offense began and ran several plays against "air," meaning there was no defense, to get warmed up.

Chase watched as JB ran the offense as the quarterback. After a couple of plays, Coach slid next to Chase on the side and told him that they were going to have him continue to play in the JV games. "We want you to get extra work and plenty of game experience. But, we also want you to be with us. So you'll practice with us during the week, play with them on Thursday, and dress out with us on Fridays."

"Okay," Chase agreed.

"Probably for the rest of the year, but we'll see how it goes. Okay?"

"Okay," Chase said again. Staying on varsity, any way they wanted him to, sounded good.

During a water break JB nodded at Chase. "I've been watching you more," the older quarterback said. "You know, you've really got a nice arm. You could use filling out a little bit, but you could be really good." Chase nodded and tried to look serious, like he heard this all the time. He was trying desperately not to smile, but could feel the corners of his mouth curl. Ugh. That was so *not cool*.

Tripp was standing nearby. "Are you saying he's a little scrawny?" he teased.

Chase squinted at Tripp, doing his best to look mean. Everyone laughed, even Chase.

Even though he'd had dinner at the Browns, he still was excited that JB was watching him and being so helpful and complimentary. Chase tried to think of something natural, something cool to say. Instead, he heard himself blurting, "Why didn't you go to Senior Skip Day?"

"Because coach told us not to. Because we're not allowed to skip school. Because that's not the right thing. I mean, for starters, anyway." JB grinned his grin, wide mouth, eyes smiling too. Chase just nodded.

"Plus," JB said, "you've gotta do the right thing, whether you think you can get away with it or not. Even if nobody knows."

The next morning, Chase noticed that Kate, who was in his English and algebra classes, seemed to be glancing at him. A lot. Or maybe he was imagining it. He tried to get Tripp's attention during English, but Mrs. Brantley noticed him before Tripp did.

"Yes, Chase. Is there something that you want to say?"

"No, ma'am. I'm fine."

He missed much of what Mrs. Brantley was saying since he kept sneaking looks back at Kate. Kate Newman. He'd certainly never spoken with her. She'd only come to Carr that year. He'd ask Hannah what she thought. Hannah was a trustworthy sister. She hadn't tried to embarrass him since they were little. Well, except for a *little* teasing every now and then.

Could Kate have known that I've been called up to the varsity? Maybe that was it. Carr wasn't the biggest school. Then again, probably not. It had just happened. But who knows? Maybe that's why she had looked at him. Yeah, that must be it.

His brain was starting to hurt from all the wondering.

After class, he walked over to her and spoke before he dwelled on it and got nervous. "I don't really know you that well, but my sister does and maybe sometime ..." and then lost his nerve. He stopped. He felt his face flush, and if he hadn't walked right over and started speaking while he was still amped up on the adrenaline and confidence of playing varsity, before he thought about what he was going to say to her, he wouldn't haven't gone up to her at all. Then again, he didn't really want to go out on a date with her. He just found himself liking her. He didn't know *what* he wanted.

She waited him out. And smiled.

He finally spoke. "Maybe sometime ... well, maybe sometime we could, like, study English together or do our reading. Or something."

"Maybe something. I think that would be nice." She was having too much fun at this. "I'm Kate."

"Yes, I know. Hannah is my sister," said Chase. "I'm Chase." She nodded. "Well, you know, maybe some reading or ..."

"I don't know how much sense it would make to read out loud," she answered, "but maybe we could study together, either for English or math." Chase pointed out that he had football practice in the afternoons so it'd have to be later, and it was her turn to be surprised.

"You play football?" So much for knowing that he'd been called up to the varsity.

After practice, Chase grabbed a quick bite at his house. *Spaghetti in the fridge*, his mom had texted. *Emergency hearing in court. Home later.* Hannah wasn't home yet, either, so he went to Tripp's house to study. Daisy lifted her head, then lowered it and fell back asleep. Another tough day of napping followed by too much pasta.

After talking football, they started homework. Chase was falling behind with trying to study so much varsity stuff on top of his JV things, and Tripp was a whiz with grammar. He just hadn't picked up algebra as fast as Chase.

"Focus on our English. After today, Mrs. Brantley is going to be watching you. What was that about, anyway?"

Chase explained how he was trying to get Tripp's attention before talking to Kate. And then mentioned how he asked her to study with him.

"You said WHAT?!" Tripp yelped, and collapsed on the floor, laughing.

Chase was still pretty embarrassed, but after a minute started laughing too. Neither one of them had even been on a date, and neither one of them really wanted to. Now, for some reason, Chase was asking to study with Kate. And embarrassing himself in the process.

They didn't finish, but it was late. Nine o'clock. He wasn't caught up yet, but he was closer in English and figured he'd just wing it in algebra.

Chase walked across the yard to his house, tossed his shoes into the garage, and headed into the kitchen, rummaging around for a snack. "Anybody home?"

There was no response for a moment, then he heard his sister's voice.

"Yes, we're here." He figured the "we" must be his mom. He'd seen her bedroom light on as he walked over. Or maybe Megan Brown. He grabbed an apple and a handful of Doritos, and headed toward his room. His room was the first on the left, but he continued down the tan carpeted hallway to Hannah's room, which was just beyond his at the end of the hall on the same side. His mother's room was across from Hannah's on the right. He and Hannah did homework either in their rooms or in the dining room. They weren't really allowed to be in Mom's office.

He knocked on Hannah's door, thinking he'd just say hi to Megan and Hannah. He planned on using the shower and wanted to warn them to use the bathroom now if they needed to. He was pretty sweaty and gross after the day's practice, but certainly Hannah and Megan had seen him at less than his best before.

Hannah answered his knock and Chase took one step into the room and froze. He tried to speak, quickly, so that he could get out of there before his face turned completely red. It was already starting to turn — he could feel the heat. Kate was there, along with Megan and Hannah.

Kate!

She shared some classes with all of them, but he'd never seen her hang out with Hannah before. She was about his height, and had that long blonde hair. Her eyes were a rather dark brown and she wore a simple dark green sweatshirt and jeans. Her cheeks had a splash of freckles. What was happening to him?

"Hi, Megan. Hi, Kate. Hey, Sis. You guys studying and stuff?" At least his voice hadn't cracked from the stress.

"Yes. But that's your only question for now. Shower first before you come ask any more questions." Hannah made a face, then grinned. And winked.

How could she tell?

He headed back to his room, frustrated and embarrassed that he hadn't had anything clever to say. *Why is it that no great things to say ever come to me when I need them to?*

As he showered, he thought of conversation starters about their algebra class or what Hannah had told him they were studying in science, a class that Kate shared with Hannah. Then he thought of a couple subtle comments he could make about football practice and spending time on the field with JB. Nothing obvious, or that made it seem that he was bragging, just a comment or two to remind them that he was now on the varsity. He really wanted to impress Kate, but knew it wouldn't be easy because, well, because ... just because.

He rushed to get dressed. He ran his fingers through his hair, and emerged from the bathroom in a long-sleeved Destroyers T-shirt and gym shorts, looking quite the athletic part, he thought. He cruised by Hannah's room, as if it was the most natural thing for him to stick his head in again, and found Hannah alone.

"She's not here," said Hannah. She smiled.

"She?" He furrowed his brow as if puzzled, trying to act like he had no idea who she was talking about. Hannah could tell he was faking.

"Kate," she said, now laughing at him. "As if we couldn't tell."

"It's that obvious?" Chase's face flushed.

"Yeah, it's that obvious. But don't worry, either she thinks it's sweet or she likes you. Either way, it's not bad."

"Thinks it's sweet?" Chase groaned. "Really? Thinks it's *sweet*?"

"Megan pointed out that you liked Kate, and Kate said she could tell. And that you are nice."

"Megan knows too? Agghh."

Hannah smiled. "It's no big deal."

Chase couldn't decide what all this meant. It sounded like maybe it was good news, as Hannah had said. But did he even want good news? Why was he wondering about her? She'd been right there tonight, but he'd missed his chance to sound clever and have interesting things to say. Instead he froze.

Again.

Who would've ever thought that getting tackled was easier than talking to girls?

CHAPTER 9

The next afternoon, Wednesday, Chase headed back out to practice.

"As I told you, participating in Skip Day meant that you would have consequences." Chase could see some of the players' shoulders slumped a little, even under their shoulder pads. "But the coaching staff and I talked."

Chase could tell that some of the guys got hopeful. Maybe Coach had changed his mind. Maybe Chase was headed back to JV and the guys who skipped would start after all. He was next to Tripp and tried to catch his eye, but couldn't. Tripp stared right at Coach.

Coach kept talking. "We decided that not only will you *run at practice*, you will *not play or dress out. At all.* You will be on the sidelines, encouraging your teammates, in regular clothes."

"But, Coach, the guys last year just ran extra sprints but didn't miss any games—" came a voice.

"No. No 'buts,'" Coach Skalaski responded. "We were going to make the punishment to *only* run, but after thinking about it, there is still a lack of responsibility that concerns us. We realized that was an insufficient punishment.

"If you skipped, we will head into battle without you. You let down your teammates, you let me down, and you let down Carr High School.

"Most of all, you have let yourselves down.

"My job is to coach football games. But why God really has me here is to prepare you for *life*. Hopefully, along the way, we'll win enough football games that I can keep my job. But whether we do or not, I have to get you ready for the rest of your lives."

JB leaned ever so slightly toward Chase and whispered quietly, "More Coach Noll quotes."

Moments later Chase found himself in the middle of practice with real parts to play on the punt protection team, the punt return team, and as a backup on the kickoff coverage and kickoff return teams. It was *really* happening; he wasn't going to play yet, but he'd be there, against the number two team in the state. Since he and Tripp had talked last week, Raines had gone up—from number three in the ratings to number two.

That night, lying in bed, he was so excited he couldn't sleep!

Chase kept reminding himself that first, he had to get through another JV game scheduled on Thursday in Gainesville. Then, he could focus on the game against Raines on Friday night. Finally, he drifted off to sleep, but it wasn't easy.

Now that he was playing on the varsity team, the JV season couldn't wrap up soon enough to satisfy Chase. They had two more games — this week and next Thursday, and then they were done and maybe he could play in a varsity game. Tonight was against Gainesville Buchholz, down in Gainesville at the local city field, Citizens Field.

Citizens Field was actually located on US 301. It was the same road that ran through Lincoln, just east of Carr High, so it was a straight shot for twenty minutes on the bus for the junior Loggerheads.

The crowds for Carr's JV games had been small even at their high point earlier in the season, and had been dwindling each week. This week the crowd was smaller still. These stands contained only a smattering of black and gold clad Buchholz parents and Loggerhead parents in blue and green. Chase didn't see any students that he recognized from Carr other than Hannah. Tripp, JB, or Megan. Or Kate. None of them were there.

As usual, the junior Loggerheads fell behind early in the game. Buchholz blocked a punt deep in Carr's territory, scoring two plays later, and then returned the next Carr punt for a touchdown. Carr's defense was otherwise playing pretty well early in the game, but their players were simply much smaller than the Class 7A school they were facing. Buchholz, with its 2,100 students, had more than twice as many students at their school. It wasn't totally fair.

That's why Coach Skalaski put them on the schedule. So that the Carr kids would improve. Chase looked over at Coach Preston, who seemed to be sweating, and not just from the heat. He looked nervous.

Their offense fought hard, but couldn't move the ball. Chase tried repeatedly to throw passes, but kept getting sacked by the defense before he could do so. In the fourth quarter, with the Bobcats leading, 20 – 0, Coach Preston had Chase repeatedly hand the ball off to Nick Wood. Running plays. They weren't going to win if they kept running the ball.

Chase grew frustrated. Utilizing their ground game here just kept the clock running and Carr would soon run out of time to score enough to win the game. Was Coach Preston even *trying* to win anymore?

He ran over to the sideline between plays and yelled to Coach Preston.

"What are we doing? Are we even trying to win?!"

Coach Preston waved him over.

"No," he said. He looked sad and kind of upset. "Coach Skalaski doesn't want you guys getting hurt — I mean, I don't either. Look, we've lost. Passing the ball means the clock stops and the game takes longer. The more you get tackled, and the other guys too. The more we run the ball with Nick instead of passing, the sooner this game will end. We could try for a miracle, but ... I'm sorry. Coach doesn't want you guys getting hurt. It's what we have to do."

Chase apologized. He understood, but at the same time, he wasn't particularly pleased at simply giving up. Minutes later, the clock was at 0:00, and they were headed back to Lincoln. The bus was quiet, as it always was following a loss. But Chase was really excited in the dark of the bus. He was almost totally done with JV and the varsity had three more regular season games, starting tomorrow night against Jacksonville Raines.

He could hardly wait.

Game Day. His first varsity game was tonight!

Chase woke up and started to climb out of bed, when he realized he was not alone.

He saw his sister's light brown hair, tussled around her pillow, lying on the floor next to his bed. Ordinarily shoulder-length, after a night's sleep it was mussed.

He sat at the edge of the bed and reached down, touching Hannah on the shoulder.

"Hannah, hey," he said softly. "We've got to get up for school."

Hannah's eyes fluttered open then closed again. She

was in her pajamas, but had no sheet, blanket, or any covers, only her pillow. "Ugh. Is it really time? I'm so tired." Her eyes still weren't open.

"Yes, it's time. Did you have that dream again?"

Hannah nodded, finally opened her eyes, and sat up. She stretched her arms, and looked at Chase with her blue eyes.

"Maybe you should switch with me or something, when this happens." He would have said that he hoped it wouldn't happen again, but he didn't think that was possible. The dream, although maybe occurring *slightly* less frequently recently, still came all too regularly. Hannah shook her head.

"I'm not gonna take your bed," she said.

"Well, maybe we should at least keep a couple of blankets in here for you to use if you need them again." He knew there was no "if" about it, but did like the thought of maybe putting that possibility into her brain. Maybe her subconscious would hear that and quit tormenting her. When it did torment her, Hannah always came looking for Chase.

Hannah had always been close to Chase, especially after their father left. Hannah was six, and Chase was five years old, turning six the next week.

They were living in Atlanta where their dad was an attorney with Frazier and Wolf, a huge law firm with offices across the country. One day, dinner had grown cold while they waited on their parents to finish talking in their bedroom. When Mom and Dad had finally come out, Dad had a suitcase in his hand, and the four of them had never eaten as a family again.

"We'd better get out to the kitchen and eat," Hannah said. "We'll get a blanket, or figure out what to do next time, later." Just then, as if on cue, their mom's voice came down the hall, calling them to get dressed and come to breakfast.

Of course, it was Daisy who had the great breakfast. She was stuffed with bacon and pancakes. Hannah was still upset, and Chase kept thinking about the game that night. As he was about to leave, his mom came in and sat down.

"You hardly ate. Are you okay? Can I get you something else? I can tell Daisy ate most of your breakfast." His mom always worried like that.

"No, I'm fine. Just excited."

"So are we. We'll be there. Can't wait to see you out there!" She kissed him on the cheek and asked again, "Are you sure there isn't something you'd eat this morning?"

"No, Mom. Thanks, though." Daisy hardly raised her head when Chase left the house. She was that *stuffed*.

Chase quickly forgot about Hannah's dream. In fact, he didn't remember a thing that was said that day in any of his classes, either. The only time he took his mind off of that night's game against Raines was when he looked over in algebra and saw Kate glance at him.

School ended, and Chase and Tripp raced home. The team was meeting back at school in an hour for their pregame meal from Morgen's BBQ. Chase's mom warned him not to have too much of the spicy barbeque sauce before the game, but she also said that he needed to *eat*. They headed into their own houses for a few minutes. Chase kicked off his shoes and lay on his bed for a while, trying to read but it was hard for him to concentrate. He was wired for the game to *just start already*!

Chase locked his bike up next to Tripp. They'd ridden back to school together and Chase followed him into the cafeteria. He didn't want to admit that he wanted Tripp to show him everything, but he suspected Tripp could tell what he was thinking, anyway. Tripp walked in first and Chase followed, looking around at the pre-game meal as other players began coming in. Guys looked a bit different this day as the seniors, most all suntanned — well, some still sun*burned* — were trickling in.

He and Tripp were at their table eating barbecue when he heard a voice. "Is this seat taken?"

JB.

Chase was thrilled to have JB wanting to sit by them. Of course, he was kind of disappointed that JB was even there. He hated to admit it, even to himself. Then again, JB seemed to always do everything the right way, and Chase realized he would have been let down if JB had disobeyed Coach as well as the principal.

"Yep, no skipping for you," said Chase by way of greeting.

JB laughed. "No chance. My parents would have killed me."

"So, you didn't want to miss the game tonight?" said Chase.

"Well, that too." JB laughed. "Apparently, you haven't met my mom and dad. Oh, wait, you did."

"They'd have killed you?" That didn't fit with what he'd seen at dinner.

"Well, no, not exactly. But they have clear rules, and we keep them. Why not? Disobedience sometimes seems harmless, but it's not. No thanks."

JB paused. "Hey, do you know all your plays for tonight, Tripp?" Chase listened while they talked about plays for a few minutes, and then he got up to head to the locker room. He had too much adrenaline to sit still any longer. He needed to be on the move.

Not only did Chase not have too much of the spicy hot sauce, he didn't have too much of anything. He was so nervous that he hardly ate at all.

Chase walked out of the school cafeteria, across the dull tile that used to be white, down the hall, and into the Carr gymnasium, decked out in blue and green. Across the basketball court, passing the girls' volleyball team. He was so focused on his steps across the wooden court that he didn't even realize that Kate and the other volleyball players were going through practice drills. As he entered the locker room, he was strangely comforted by the musty smell of sweat hanging in the air in the heat of the locker room in the middle of fall.

He found his blue jersey with green numbers — they had given him number three, thankfully — and he began to put on the rest of his uniform. His locker was in between numbers one and four. Megan Brown wore number two and dressed in her own locker room, over in the girls volleyball and girls basketball locker room. He sat in his cramped locker for a few minutes, despite it being made of unforgiving metal. It was really hard and uncomfortable, but today he didn't notice. He had never sat in it before because it was too hard, but today he did. He listened to Lecrae on his MP3 player and took deep breaths. Lecrae, his new favorite, after the dinner at the Browns' house.

Other players, including Tripp and then JB, began filing in while he continued to sit in his locker.

He finally walked out of the locker room, trotting onto the field with Tripp for pregame warmups. The sun had set, and the temperature had finally started to drop. A little, anyway. The Raines Vikings players were lined up on the far sideline, and as big as Chase thought that his new varsity teammates were, the Raines players were even bigger.

It looked like the uniform trucks at Ohio State and the Minnesota Vikings had collided. Raines wore white jerseys with red numerals, and dark red pants trimmed in gray, looking just like Ohio State. Their helmets were a deep red, also, with a silver Viking horn on each side, like the Minnesota Vikings.

Along with their size, it was a daunting sight.

Coach Skalaski gathered the team in the locker room one final time before they headed out for the opening kickoff. Chase, along with the rest of the twenty-eight guys who were dressed out, was kneeling on one knee, resting his elbow on his other knee, looking straight at Coach.

"Guys, this is a good team. There is a reason they are undefeated and ranked number two in the state. They are good. They're big and they're fast and they're strong.

"But I'm not asking you to do anything amazing. Champions do the little things well, they don't have to do the extraordinary things. If you'll just do the ordinary things over and over, that you are capable of doing, we'll be just fine.

"After all, we've had some success ourselves this year" — unlike the JV version of the Loggerheads, the varsity team was rolling along, at 7 – 0, ranked number five in the state — "and we've gotten there by doing the ordinary things better than anyone else."

Apparently they didn't do enough of the ordinary things very well that night.

Raines had everything that you would expect out

of a team ranked that highly. The quarterback was not as big as JB, but he was a good passer. He spread his passes around to several different receivers, all of whom could run and had good hands catching the ball.

Raines won easily. The stands were full, because Raines brought lots of fans to go along with all of the Carr supporters. Being a home game, most of the fans in attendance were in blue and green, and most left the stadium disappointed.

In spite of the loss, JB's rushing totals were especially amazing. It made sense since Carr had a lot of trouble blocking Raines and keeping them away from JB. Too many of Carr's starting offensive line were in regular clothes on the sideline, so the younger replacements, like Solomon, were outmatched. Coach moved his best lineman, Will Kingston, from Left Guard to his brother's position of Right Tackle in an effort to shore up the right side of the line, but Carr's line still couldn't protect JB. In addition to the seniors, Chris Kingston had tagged along to St. Augustine Beach, even though he was only a junior. His absence was sorely missed as well and as a result, JB was running for his life much of the night, being chased by the Raines defense.

Chase was excited, even though they lost. He hadn't played, but it was thrilling to be out there in front of the big crowd and bright lights.

Coach Skalaski gathered the team in the locker room following the 35–9 loss, and took a different approach than what Chase expected. He figured Coach would be angry. Chase was wrong. Every time Chase had seen him talk, he was trying to keep them sharp, pep them up. He did again, but not how Chase thought. Coach Skalaski could see tonight that his team needed a big pat on the back.

"Wow. They're pretty good, aren't they? But, then again, so is Megan Brown." He tossed a football toward Megan, who grinned, and then tried to look embarrassed. After all, she didn't want to look *too* happy after a big loss.

"Three field goals. *All* of our points. Made all of her attempts, and two of them were from over forty yards!" Megan had made kicks of 30, 41, and 44 yards. "At this rate, when she's a senior, she'll probably be making 70-yarders!"

The team cheered.

"Listen up, y'all. When we put Raines on the schedule, we weren't sure if we could make it through the season undefeated. We knew they would be a good test for us. And that was with our full roster — *all* of our players. We were missing *seven* guys tonight — a lot of them starters, good players. I'm proud of you all, you fought, you battled, you scrapped. JB, my word. Young man, you were on the run all night, and are just a remarkable player."

Everyone cheered again.

Coach Skalaski quieted them back down. "But the

rest of you did some good things out there too. There will be some things that the coaches and I will see on film that we will point out to you that we can do better, of course.

"But I love the effort. And it was an important lesson — more important than going undefeated this year — learning how to deal with adversity. And there's no doubt, we're not done with adversity. I'm sure it will be back. And how we deal with it will define us as a team and as young people."

None of the team realized how right Coach Skalaski was, or how much adversity would ultimately test them. For Chase and Tripp, what lay on the horizon would put their friendship to the test.

CHAPTER 10

The tapping was quiet but urgent on Chase's bedroom window. He was still groggy but quickly scooted over to the window even as he came awake. He stuck a couple of fingers between the blinds and lifted them up far enough to see out, figuring it had to be Tripp. Tripp was the only person who tapped on his bedroom window. Plus, Daisy wasn't barking. In fact, she'd gone back to sleep on his bed after lifting her head.

Sure enough, Tripp had his face pressed against the glass.

"Are you ready?" Tripp asked through the windowpane.

"Not quite. My alarm didn't go off." Chase realized in his tired state that he'd forgotten to set it, since it was usually his mom who woke him up on Sunday mornings for church. "I'll be right there." Chase raced around the room, dressed in a pair of jeans and a gray and black

T-shirt with "Destroyers" printed across the front and raced outside. Tripp and his dad were waiting for him.

"Chase, old buddy, we're going to see the Tampa Bay Pirates play the Indianapolis Mustangs. You probably don't want to wear the Destroyers shirt. It's okay to take a minute — we'll wait for you." Mr. Stevens grinned as he spoke.

Chase face-palmed himself, pivoted on his toe, and headed back inside, trying not to wake his sister or his mom. He found a neutral bright blue golf shirt and before long they were on the highway, heading south, talking about all kinds of things on the three-and-a-half-hour drive down from Lincoln to Tampa. College and pro football, the World Series that had just ended, and school. And girls, but only a little.

Chase really enjoyed hanging around Tripp and his dad. It made him feel, well, more like he had a dad around too.

Eventually they took the Martin Luther King Jr. Drive exit off of Interstate 275, and headed a couple of miles to the stadium. Mr. Stevens pulled into a parking lot in the shadow of Raymond James Stadium, less than fifty yards from the entrance.

"Wow. This is a great place to park," Chase remarked. Tripp and his dad nodded.

"I think it's because all of the pro teams have to send scouts back and forth to visit each other," Tripp said. "If they send a lousy pass to you — or don't send one at all — they figure a lousy parking pass will be sent back to them as well. At least, that's my guess. We've always had great parking at these games. But I guess Dad would have more experience."

"Yes," said Mr. Stevens. "I think that's exactly it. We all send good parking passes to each other. Even the colleges send us good parking passes, because they know it would be easy enough for us to skip their game, and head to another school. If we skipped their games enough, we might not draft as many of their players — we wouldn't have seen them play."

Mr. Stevens reached across into the back seat and grabbed the light windbreakers that they had thrown in at the last minute. Clouds were rolling in, and cooler air had finally settled in across Tampa. "A number of times we'll have flights to catch or we'll have to drive to a second game, so we're always on a time crunch. If there's another option that's more convenient, we may end up taking that one instead. And colleges, even though they might protest about pros hanging around and distracting their players, know that their players love having pro scouts hanging around." Chase nodded.

By now, they were approaching the gate, and as the security officers were signing them in, Mr. Stevens handed the boys their Official Passes. Tripp looped the string on the pass through one of his belt loops, and Chase, watching Tripp, did the same.

"Where's our ticket?"

Tripp smiled. "This is it. This gets you anywhere, anytime. The Official ones do."

Chase was full of questions. "Is this a gate? I don't see any other fans coming this way." They'd always used tickets and gone through a regular gate in Jacksonville.

"No," replied Mr. Stevens. He looked back down the hallway toward the table where they had checked in. "This is the entrance for the media — sportswriters and broadcasters and stuff — and also for the players, coaches, and their families. Michael had told me to come in this entrance before — it's easier."

During the drive, Tripp's dad told them that Michael Lamberson was one of his teammates from college, and was now the general manager of the Pirates. It was hard to believe that there were already thousands of people in the building, because it looked totally empty. They continued down the deserted hallway. As they reached a connecting hallway, Mr. Stevens held a hand out on either side for Trip and Chase to stop before entering the new, wider hallway. "Hang on, guys. You've always got to keep your head on a swivel around stadiums — you know, look in every direction. Just like on a football field!"

He took a small step in the hallway with Chase and Tripp following behind, and they immediately saw why. A golf cart carrying bags of ice whizzed by them on the left. A man with a walkie-talkie ran past.

Mr. Stevens said, "Come on!" and headed to the

right. Before long, they passed a sign that said "Pirates Locker Room," and Chase saw one of the Pirates linemen walk out into the hallway. He was huge. Just huge. They followed him, and took a left down a short ramp which opened up onto the field.

The sky was still gray, probably just as gray as it had been, but it seemed lighter, since they had been underneath the stadium for the last five minutes. They walked out onto the field, and Mr. Stevens led them down the sideline, where they stood over to the side and watched warmups.

Tripp's dad pulled out a stopwatch and a small recorder, and began timing punts and speaking notes on his general observations about players. Things like "Thirty-five drops his hips well when he comes out of his break," and "Fourteen has a slight limp, possibly the left knee." And so on.

Chase turned to Tripp. "What's he doing?"

"He's looking for anything that won't show up when the coaches watch the game film. The Destroyers play the Pirates in two weeks, so anything he can see will help the coaches. Like number thirty-five, David, is a rookie and may not play today, so there won't be any film on him. And number fourteen, Hicks, looks hurt. So if he doesn't play well, the coaches may want to know he was playing hurt."

"So can he stop when the game starts?"

"Not really," Tripp answered.

They thought Mr. Stevens wasn't paying attention to them but he called over his shoulder, "Nope. Gotta keep working while you guys are in the press box eating hot dogs."

"Yeah, during the game he'll be watching the sidelines to try and learn any signals the teams might use — those won't be on film, either."

"It's against the rules to videotape the sidelines." Tripp's dad jumped into the conversation again.

"Really? I didn't know that," Chase said.

"Most fans don't," Tripp responded. "Most people had never heard of it until the Boston Minutemen got in trouble a few years ago for doing that."

Chase nodded. He remembered hearing about that. Thirty minutes later the teams headed back to the locker room and Mr. Stevens led them off the field and up past the Pirates locker room. They entered an elevator and minutes later, Chase was in the Press Box. Rows and rows of low counters with desk chairs so the reporters could use their computers or notebooks and write while they watched. Mr. Stevens checked a chart on the wall in the back of the room.

"Come on. We're over here, seats thirty-one, thirty-two, and thirty-three." They settled in and by the time they'd reached halftime, Chase had decided it was the perfect way to watch a game. Sitting in a padded chair at a long counter, where reporters typed on laptops — *there was Mike Garafolo!* — watching through a huge window, eating hot dogs and chips from a buffet with an all-you-can-drink soda machine. Tripp had warned him that no cheering — for either team — was allowed in the press box, and Chase had made sure not to make a sound.

He did find plenty to eat, though. Bags of chips and unlimited root beer. At halftime the boys ate hot dogs and found themselves at the next table over from Mike Garafolo — again! — and Peter King, two of the best-known NFL writers!

The next thing he knew, it was the end of the third quarter and Chase was on the edge of his seat. He didn't really have a favorite of these two teams, and the Mustangs had just tied the score, 17 – 17. The Pirates were moving the ball trying to take the lead again, and the home crowd was getting more enthusiastic.

Mr. Stevens began packing up his papers. "You guys about ready? Probably five minutes until we leave," he said. Tripp nodded.

Chase leaned over to Tripp, bewildered. "Why? It's just getting good."

"Scouts never stay until the end. They always beat traffic and get home — or to the airport," Tripp said.

Mr. Stevens overheard them. "Actually, now that I think about it, today it doesn't matter. We're just heading home after this. Getting stuck in traffic wouldn't matter. Do you want to stay?"

Chase paused and looked toward Tripp.

Tripp's dad smiled. "We should stay, right, guys?" Chase nodded. "Yes, sir. Please." Tripp shrugged, then nodded. He'd been to lots of professional games.

Tripp's dad sat back. "Let's go ahead and stay at least for a while longer. Chase, text your mom and make sure it's okay if we stay later than I told her." Chase's mom replied that it was fine, and forty-five minutes later, the Pirates wrapped up a dramatic win and the happy hometown fans walked out of the stadium alongside Chase, Tripp, and Mr. Stevens.

"What a great way to watch a game!" exclaimed Chase. He was glad he hadn't worn his Destroyers shirt.

"Sure is. Except did you notice how little I actually saw?" Tripp's dad asked. Chase thought about it and nodded. Tripp's dad added, "Plus, today is the first time in forever that I've stayed around until the end. That's what I meant when I said that what I do was a bad job for a football fan." Chase nodded, thoughtfully. "I'm always taking notes, writing things down during the most exciting parts, and then leaving early. Most fans think my job is cool but they'd be happier just buying a ticket."

Chase agreed and climbed into the back seat. Before they got out of the snarl of cars in the parking lot, he'd fallen asleep. He woke up in Lincoln as Mr. Stevens pulled into the driveway.

CHAPTER 11

By Wednesday, Chase could feel that he was falling behind in school. He'd done a little homework on Saturday, but none on Sunday when they went to the Pirates game in Tampa. Mondays were a normal day off for JV, but this Monday afternoon meant meetings with the varsity watching film and learning plays, and Tuesday's practice was uneventful but time consuming. And this was all after two games—JV and varsity—on Thursday and Friday of the week before. This was the last week that he had to make it work, but he could feel himself slipping behind, especially in math.

The Raines game was long behind them, thank goodness, and the JV season was winding down. The final game was this week. Chase was ready to focus fully on varsity football. Well, varsity football and his school work. His studies had suffered, he had to admit. Hopefully it would improve. He *was* catching up in English, although it was to the detriment of algebra. He hadn't cracked open the algebra book in a week, and he was a little fuzzy about what Mr. Payne was talking about in class. Oh well, he'd figure it out later.

Today they were practicing on an open grassy field behind the student parking lot beside the stadium. Wednesdays were usually their most physical practice days with the most blocking and tackling, and Coach Skalaski did not want them to rip up the grass on the stadium field. The practice field was lined, like the game field, but it was only sixty-five yards long instead of one hundred, and didn't have any goal posts.

It was more than fine for most everything, but Tripp told Chase that Coach liked to paint the picture of David vs. Goliath when he talked about their practice field. How rough they had it while other schools had big, beautiful locker rooms and practice fields.

"Somehow, I'm thinking that he's exaggerating, a little. But what do I know?" Tripp had said.

"Bring it in, guys," Coach Skalaski yelled, and the players gathered around him in the middle of the open field before practice.

Forty guys standing and kneeling around Coach Skalaski nodded or murmured their excitement.

"Let's try that again. You don't have to yell it, but at

least be firm and resolute. You guys know what resolute means?"

Everyone was silent until JB spoke up. "It means unwavering, and I'm guessing Coach Noll said it. A lot." Coach laughed.

"Funny guy, JB. Is everyone clear? Resolute means standing strong."

A strong, "Yes, sir" resounded across the field.

It sounded, well, *resolute*, thought Chase.

"Good, now let me say one thing about Scout Team and how they'll be helping us out come Friday night. Myself, Coach Parker, Coach Quinn, and Coach Martin will all be putting you in places where you will be doing what *the other team will be doing* on Friday night. Your job is to pretend to be the other team in practice. Because of that, a good Scout Team does what they are told. It is critically important that you give us a good look at what we will be seeing. If you know the play that we are running, or can tell where the ball is going to go, you are *not* to make a play on it, unless that is what you've been instructed to do.

"Just do what you're told," Coach emphasized.

He turned to Chase in front of the team. Chase gulped. "Let me give you an example. Chase, we are going to put you at safety on our defensive scout team." Chase nodded.

"When that happens, Coach Parker will tell you where Bartram Trail's safety will be positioned, and then whether he initially takes a step back or comes up to tackle a runner or whatever the situation is. So you have to do *exactly* that. Even if you hear JB audible — call out — to a play that you know and know where the ball is going to go, that is an advantage you have that the players against us *will not have* on Friday. So, I need you to forget what you know and think and react as if you were *actually* the Bartram safety. Does that make sense? Pretend that you don't know."

Chase nodded. It did make sense.

They split up a few minutes later and Chase began running drills with JB and Roger Dalton. Roger was like an older version of Tripp, with sandy blond hair, blue eyes, and a tanned surfer face, but was far more laid-back and self-assured than Tripp. And not as nice. Chase stayed calm on the outside but would get worked up inside, but Roger looked calm everywhere, inside and out.

The three quarterbacks loosened up by throwing easy passes, then started drills. Since there were only two regular centers to snap the ball, Chase watched as Roger and JB took five snaps each, then worked on their footsteps as they took five-step drops as if they were going to pass. Then the centers left to catch up with the rest of the offensive line for their individual drills, while the running backs and tight ends came over to join the three quarterbacks. Chase tried to get into a regular rotation with the other two but Roger made it difficult. Chase did throw a few short passes to the running backs and tight ends.

"Hey, Squirt's got a good arm," said Roger, grinning. Chase cringed at "Squirt." Roger wasn't all that tall himself, but his 5-foot-11-inch frame was significantly different — broader — than Chase's skinny 5-foot-7-inches. Both of them were dwarfed by JB, however.

"Yeah," said JB. "I've seen him sling it before — he can throw." Now Chase was beaming. He was glad because he didn't think that anybody could see the huge smile that lit up inside his helmet.

Later in practice, JB and Roger were still working with the offense, while Chase was positioned as the Bartram Trail Bears safety. Coach Parker told him to take two steps back initially on each play, and then drift in whichever direction the quarterback was rolling, and to not let any of the receivers get behind him. Easy enough. Eventually, he got a little bored, and while he was trying to listen to the coaches on the field, he wasn't totally paying attention. He was catching snippets of them giving instruction.

"Drew, with two receivers on both sides, you've got to talk."

"Run it again. Run it again. On the line."

"Dimitri, this is big." Chase started listening more carefully as they were talking to Dimitri Anderson, a wide receiver, who was struggling to block downfield as a running back came up behind him. "If you block it right, this play could go a long way." They ran the play again, and Dimitri was able to block better, like Tripp was doing on the other side. Chase nodded. That play *could* go a long way.

But on the next play, Roger Dalton dropped a shot-gun snap.

"Stop! Stop! Stop! Get back on it! Get back on the ball, run it, men, one more time! This is *our play* this week, we've got to get it right."

Then, just as soon as Roger caught the next snap, Coach whistled the players to stop. "Chris, get in your stance. No, Chris, stand up. Look at Will. That's what I want, now get in your stance. You got it? No, get up. Look at Will again. Now you got it? In your stance. Better."

Some of the stuff was downright funny. Especially since it wasn't being directed at Chase, and he could stay in the back and just watch. One player, Jackson Parker, had somehow shaved the word "Anytime" into the left side of his head.

Fairly cool, Chase thought. Not for Chase to have in his hair, but for Jackson, anyway. Except Jackson kept coming off the field during practice. He strained his calf, and then twisted his ankle, and then his wrist was tight. Off and on and then off and then on again. And then his finger was jammed. Finally, on his sixth trip off the field in the twenty plays that they ran in the "Team" session, Coach Quinn yelled across the field.

"Why does your hair say 'Anytime,' if you keep coming out? Maybe it should say *Sometime* or *No Time*." Everyone laughed, except for Jackson. He turned, and headed back onto the field. "Bad" ankle, wrist, calf, finger, and all.

Chase paid for his lack of focus after a while. He heard Roger audible out of a running play and into a deep passing play, and on instinct, got to the spot that he knew the ball would be thrown to, and made a leaping catch for an interception.

An interception! On the varsity! He was so excited. *And against Roger!*

Rather than hearing praise come from the coaches, his excitement immediately vanished as he heard Coach Skalaski yell, "Chase, that's exactly what I was warning you about! *Don't* do it *again*! The Bartram safety would have been fooled and closing to support the run. Not dropping back and rolling over to where you were. It never would have been an interception on Friday — that's not fair! Run it again!" Chase's face flushed, and he was glad for the facemask that covered some of that up.

Chase and Tripp spoke after practice, as they rode their bikes home. "So, what's Bartram Trail like? Their record isn't very good," said Chase. "An easy win for us?"

Tripp responded, "I think Bartram will be really good. It's a lot bigger school than us. They've been losing to some of the really huge schools around here.

Four wins, three losses doesn't seem so bad then if you look at it that way. We think Coach Skalaski set the schedule up this way. We've already played all of our five district games. We beat Palatka, Keystone Heights, Umatilla, Weeki Wachee, and somebody else. I forget who the other district game was."

"Bushnell, or Sumter County — whatever they're called," Chase said. "It was one of the games I didn't make it to. It wasn't that long ago."

"Oh yeah," said Tripp. "North Sumter. So, anyway, we've made the playoffs, as Coach hoped. So these last few games are just getting us ready for the play-offs. Raines, Bartram, and then Union County. I mean, I know we play Union every year, and they're a smaller school than we are, but they're always really good. So all three of these are basically playoff warmup games. He didn't say this, but I don't think that he thinks we'll win."

"Okay. Well, I'll see ya, Thug."

"Yeah, see ya tomorrow, Thug."

CHAPTER 12

The days were passing with a blur. Time was flying by. Algebra, science, English, art, American history, and PE. Then practice. Then homework as best as he could squeeze it in. Most days, he was hanging out with Tripp talking football.

His mom walked through the kitchen, with Hannah behind her.

"Hannah, put your stuff in the car, why don't you? I'll be right there." Hannah walked into the garage, and Chase's mom sat down next to him at the table. It wasn't a court day, apparently. She looked nice but not totally fancy. Daisy lowered her head from next to Chase's arm and tried to look invisible. Like she wasn't waiting for more breakfast.

"Honey, I'm concerned about your grades. It seems

like you've been spending an awful lot of time at practice and two games a week and—"

"I'm doing fine, Mom." This was true. Chase's grades were still good, mainly because he hadn't had any tests recently, since he started playing both JV and varsity.

"Really?" Mrs. Clark's look was serious, and steady. Chase knew rule number one in their house had always been *tell the truth*.

"Yes, my grades are still really good." It was totally true. She didn't ask if he was falling behind, only about his grades.

Mrs. Clark sat back and thought. "Okay, but are you keeping up? Even if your grades are good, how is your schoolwork?" Sometimes it wasn't easy having a lawyer for a mother.

"Well, it's been pretty busy ..."

"That's what I think. I'm surprised they're asking you to go to both games. I'm going to call Coach Skalaski and talk with him about it. You need to put your studies first."

"No, Mom! Please don't call! It'll be fine. Tonight is our last JV game — then it's a normal schedule. There's no point in calling Coach!" Chase wanted badly to keep playing varsity, even into the playoffs. He didn't think that having his mom call the coach would help that.

Mrs. Clark stood. "Okay, I won't call yet but we'll talk again, soon. I'm trusting that things will get better. It's just been too much for you, I think."

"Okay, we'll talk. No problem. Things'll get easier, soon. I'll catch back up."

That evening, Chase played his last JV game for the year, and he hoped, forever. The JV Loggerheads were trying to avoid going 1 – 6 as a final record for their season. On the sideline, Coach Preston was sweating. Literally sweating. And for the first time in a while, he needn't have been, as it was sixty-five degrees, a pleasant late October evening. Nice and cool.

They were playing the Mandarin Mustangs, a team from South Jacksonville, and late in the game, the Carr JV trailed 35 – 19.

Mandarin was about to punt. Chase tried to rally the offense. He was ready to lead and wanted them to sense that he was their leader — he wanted to feel it as well, the way the great quarterbacks did.

"We're gonna get the ball in great field position. We're gonna score, get it back, and score again and tie it up." The other players got pumped, screaming, "Yes, yes!"

Just then, Mandarin's punter, who was having a terrible day already, kicked yet another lousy punt. The ball was low, turning end over end, spinning wildly, and bounced at the Mandarin 40-yard line, heading for Nick at midfield.

"Peter! Peter!" Nick yelled, the usual call from punt returners, which meant that the punt had been poorly kicked. When a receiving team heard "Peter," they knew to clear out of the area so that the ball wouldn't take a funny bounce and hit them by accident. If that happened it was a live ball and it was anybody's for the taking. If the ball goes untouched, the receiving team gets it wherever it settles.

And then, for some reason, Nick tried to field the bouncing ball and return it. Not really a good idea. It slipped off his fingers!

Nick turned toward the loose, bouncing ball, but was immediately hit by a Mandarin player and knocked away from the fumble. Mandarin players began yelling "Ball! Ball!" to indicate a fumble and one of their orange jerseys leapt on it.

Chase groaned. So much for the confident field general leading his team to victory.

Carr's JV finished 1 – 6, and as they headed for the bus, Chase noticed that the temperature had dropped and he was actually chilly.

Friday, the next day, Chase felt like he was holding his breath all day at school. His stomach was in knots. On the way to school he'd asked Tripp, "Do you think I'll stay on varsity?"

Tripp had been puzzled. "Why not?"

"Well, because all the Senior Skip Day guys are back. You know, Roger is back to being the second quarterback, and the others too. Maybe Coach won't even need us for practice."

Tripp tried to make Chase feel better. "Yes, I'm sure

you will. I mean, why let you practice with the varsity all week only to change something on gameday? Coach Skalaski wouldn't do that."

Chase figured Tripp was right and while they were locking their bikes up, Tripp told Chase he worried too much. Still, Chase was anxious as he headed to first period, and through most of the day, hoping that Coach wouldn't decide that he didn't need him, Solomon, Nick, or the other JV guys on the varsity any longer.

Nobody kicked him out of pre-game meal, and he boarded the bus that afternoon. No one tapped him on the shoulder to get off.

They were on the bus headed away from Carr, driving toward Bartram Trail High School, when Tripp caught his eye.

"Told you," he mouthed.

Chase made a face at him. But he was glad Tripp was right.

The drive to Bartram Trail High School didn't take long from Lincoln. Straight out to the east, toward the beach, then tucked away in the trees in a new development south of Jacksonville. It wasn't too far from where his grandparents had moved when they'd left Lincoln.

Carr had a good week of practice to prepare, but it wasn't enough. Bartram Trail was even bigger and faster than Raines, and the game didn't go particularly well. JB threw some nice passes and ended up rushing for almost one hundred and fifty yards, but Will and Chris Kingston and the rest of the offensive line couldn't protect him long enough for him to get off many decent passes. Most of his running plays were supposed to be passes, but time and again he was scrambling for positive yardage while trying to avoid getting hit.

So much for that! Chase was just happy that JB didn't get hurt along the way considering all the times that he was tackled by the Bartram players. For as big as Raines looked the week before, Bartram looked like a college team.

Late in the third quarter, Chase stood on the sideline watching. JB was one tough player. As the o-line collapsed, he avoided a sack and made an incredible throw toward Tripp. Tripp caught the pass right in front of Chase. He was immediately tackled by a Bartram defensive back. It was a brutal hit. And Chase had a front-row seat. Bartram's defender got to his feet and headed back onto the field while Tripp lay at Chase's feet for a moment. Chase reached down to help him up. He realized Tripp's eyes were closed. It was the longest moment of Chase's life.

"Tripp!" he called. Chase felt like his heart stopped. Was Tripp breathing? He'd never seen him like that.

Tripp's eyes fluttered open and Chase took a deep breath. *Whew. Tripp was okay.* He helped Tripp up.

"Why are you here, Chase?" Tripp asked. "Didn't JV have a game this week?" Chase looked for Tripp's usual goofy grin, showing that he was messing with Chase — although Chase didn't find it very funny. There was no smile from Tripp. He was serious.

Coach Skalaski and Todd, the team's trainer, rushed over seconds later. Tripp was standing, but looked like he was swaying to Chase. Unsteady on his feet, like he might just fall over sideways.

Todd spoke to Tripp. "Are you okay? Why don't you lie back down and let's take a look at you."

"I'm fine," said Tripp. "I'm fine." Coach and Todd turned to Chase.

"Is he fine, Chase?" Coach asked.

Chase hesitated. "I'm sure he is. I'm sure whatever he said is right."

Coach and Todd looked at each other, then at Chase. Then they looked back at Tripp.

"Figure it out, Todd," Coach said. "But be careful with him." Coach headed back over toward the offense, and Todd nodded and slowly walked Tripp over to the bench. He was always careful with the players. He wanted Carr to win, but his first job was to keep everyone healthy and safe.

Todd motioned for Chase to follow him over near Tripp. Todd watched Tripp walk. He was moving gingerly, as if the ground was shifting slightly with every step.

He put Tripp through some concussion tests.

Doctors from the University of Florida's hospital had come over before the season and talked to the coaches and players about the dangers of a concussion, a brain bruise. Todd had learned tests to give, and the players had been told to always tell Todd and their coaches if anything felt wrong with their head. That's when they'd told the players about having to sit out for two weeks after a concussion — maybe longer.

After the tests, Todd looked from Tripp to Chase. "I can't tell," Todd said.

"I'm fine," said Tripp. "I can go back in. I don't have any problems."

Todd looked back at Chase. "Chase, tell me, what did you see? Did Tripp lose consciousness? Or did he say anything weird?"

Chase paused. He knew the right answer. Tripp had been knocked out, and when he came back to reality, it wasn't really reality. Tripp didn't even know why Chase was standing over him. They'd had conversations for weeks about Chase playing varsity, and now Tripp didn't even know Chase was on the team. Even though Tripp had been telling him all day not to worry about staying on varsity.

As Chase thought, Tripp was looking at Chase, pleading silently with his eyes. Begging. His shaggy blond hair was sweaty, matted and all messed up, and his eyes still looked somewhat wild to Chase, who had known him for so long. They looked watery and red.

Chase thought of their friendship. He knew that Tripp would do what was best for him — but what was that? Let him keep playing or tell the truth? With a concussion, Tripp would be out for two weeks, at least. Their final regular season game, plus the first playoff game.

In his heart, Chase knew the right thing to do. *Tell the truth.* He gulped.

"He was unconscious," Chase said. "And then he was confused. He didn't even know why I was there on the sideline before I helped him up."

Tripp glared at Chase, then hung his head.

Todd picked up Tripp's helmet, so that Tripp couldn't go back into the game, and walked off to talk with Coach Skalaski.

Tripp glared at Chase, turned on his heel, and walked away without a word.

Chase watched him go.

CHAPTER 13

Chase was awakened the next morning by a hand gently shaking his shoulder.

"Chase, I need you to get up. We need to leave in a few minutes." He opened his eyes to see his mom above him, waking him up.

"Is everything okay?" Chase asked.

"Yes," his mom said. "I've just got to go into the office today. I figured you could go with me."

"Where's Hannah?"

"Still in bed. She's probably going to Megan's later. Why don't you just go with me? I'd like for you to. You could do homework. You could catch up." Chase groaned. This happened every now and then, his mom working on a Saturday. If he stayed home he'd be stranded — except for his bike — and if he went, he'd be stranded at her office too.

"You can walk around campus. Plus, you need some new shoes. Later today we could head over to the mall in Gainesville." Hmm. *This* was more enticing.

He was torn. The slim shopping choices meant, unless you wanted to shop at Wal-Mart in Lincoln, that you had to head to Gainesville or Jacksonville. He didn't mind Wal-Mart usually, but he'd already looked for shoes there and didn't find any, well, *cool* enough. He rubbed his eyes, and could see the sunlight was straining to get in and around the blinds on his bedroom window. It looked like a bright morning already even for the early hour. He looked at the clock. Oh. It wasn't so early. 8:15 already. No wonder the sun was so bright.

"Why don't you get dressed? I'm going to take off soon."

Chase thought for a moment. "Thanks, but I think I'll head over to Tripp's. He was pretty mad last night. Maybe we can hang out together—that'd be good."

Hannah and his mom knew the whole story from the car ride home, about Tripp being tackled, Chase telling the truth, and then Tripp ignoring him until he was taken to the hospital to get checked out.

His mom thought for a moment. "Okay, why don't you head over to Tripp's soon? Maybe I'll wait and go in an hour—there are some things I still need to do here first."

Minutes later he headed over. He didn't bother to

shower, but instead threw on a Gator hat, and he and Daisy walked next door.

Kayla answered the door. "Hi, Chase!" Her face lit up in a smile. "Come on in!" Mrs. Stevens came in from the kitchen and gave him a hug.

"I know Tripp was mad, but I appreciate what you did," she said. Chase was relieved.

"So Tripp isn't still mad?" he asked.

"Well ... I don't know. He didn't tell us the story. In fact, he didn't talk to us at all last night even though they made him stay awake all night so they could watch him. They kept him at the hospital overnight and Kayla and I stayed in the room with him. Finally at five this morning they let us bring him home, so we did."

"Then how do you ..."

"Your mom told us about it late last night." She smiled again at Chase, and he realized how tired she looked.

"Can I talk to Tripp?"

She shook her head. "I'm afraid he isn't up yet." At first, Chase was surprised, because Tripp was a really early riser. Then again, he'd been up most of the night. Mrs. Stevens continued talking. "The doctor told us that after he'd stayed awake for so long that once he got home, we could let him sleep. But since he wouldn't talk, we couldn't tell. He seemed okay—just didn't want to talk."

"Okay, well, will you have him call when he gets up?"

She shook her head no. "Actually, he's supposed to stay quiet today, so I really shouldn't."

"That sounds awful!" Chase exclaimed.

She nodded. "Maybe tomorrow or Monday will be more normal. They want him to start exercising his brain. It's like rehab for another body part, like a muscle sprain. The doctor is supposed to let us know later." Chase left, and the bad feeling in the pit of his stomach had returned. He really wanted to talk to Tripp.

He and Daisy entered the house and his mom was waiting.

"Why don't you get ready and we'll go?"

"You knew?"

"Pretty much," she said. "They said he'd have to stay quiet today. Were you able to see him first?"

Chase shook his head but didn't say anything. He was frustrated and upset. He didn't want to cry in front of her.

"Come on. It'll be a distraction," his mom said.

His mom's office was on the side street of 2nd Avenue across 13th Street, on the edge of the University of Florida campus. She'd had this office for the last couple of years. It was a simple office with off-white walls, a painting of the beach, and a nice carpet. There were a limited number of law books—most legal research occurred online over the Internet these days—and Cindy Clark thought keeping your shoes looking nice was the key to success. Chase supposed that she applied the same reasoning to offices and carpeting.

Chase didn't come as often anymore now that he and Tripp could stay home alone. Hanging out in the office alone wasn't his idea of how to spend a Saturday, but he also enjoyed the bustle of campus, the college kids always rushing somewhere. He and Tripp had come over three or four times together before, and he'd wandered around campus once with Hannah too. But to be without Tripp or Hannah...

Tripp. Ugh.

In her office Chase got himself a bottle of water from the refrigerator and headed toward the door. "I'm gonna head out for a little while and look around campus," he said.

"You don't want to do any studying?"

"Not yet," he replied. "I'll wander for a while and come back and do it then."

"That's fine. Just remember to stay in public places — out in the open."

"I know, Mom," Chase sighed. Even as he sighed, he knew that he was pretty lucky that she let him explore campus on his own. Of course, it may have only been because she knew he was upset about Tripp. "How long do you think you'll be working?" he asked.

"Probably until right after lunch — maybe a little earlier. You can text or call if you want to check in."

He slipped out and crossed 13th Street, wearing his orange Gator hat along with a green Carr Loggerheads sweatshirt.

So much for the bustle of campus. It was pretty quiet at 10:00 am on a Saturday morning. The Gators football team was playing at Auburn that night, Chase remembered, and so campus was still sleepy and silent.

He walked past the brick buildings, many of which had been there for generations, the typical state school look. Three, four, and five-story, sprawling orange-red brick buildings. He liked being on campus. It was full of oak and pine trees, and always held mystery around the next corner. He and Tripp would imagine them-selves as students — or really better yet as Gator ath-letes — strutting across campus. Every time he was on campus, there were just so many different people of different types that nobody thought they looked par-ticularly out of place, even as thirteen-year-olds. Today felt weird, being by himself.

Chase headed past the university's main administra-tion building into the heart of the college. He walked past the buildings that made up the business school and through the Plaza of the Americas, a grassy open area in front of the main library. The library was probably deserted on a Saturday morning, but Chase finally saw students on the green of the Plaza, playing Frisbee golf outside. He figured they thought there was always time for the library later. He dodged a Frisbee and slipped around Century Tower, one of the most prominent landmarks of the university and into The Hub, a main hangout and lunch spot for students. He bought a Sprite instead of a Starbucks — his mom constantly reminded him that coffee would stunt his growth — because, at the heart of it, he didn't like coffee. Plus, that was one of her pet peeves, kids drinking coffee.

Chase enjoyed time on campus with the activity and constant action — the college-age girls always walking around wearing orange and blue. Waiting to pay for his drink, Chase stood behind a college girl wearing a T-shirt with three triangles, whatever that meant. Probably a math shirt, he figured. Not surprisingly, she didn't give the thirteen-year-old behind her a second glance.

What a bummer, being here without Tripp. Usually, they would wander through the bookstore and then to the football stadium. If there were games going on, they'd sit out and watch baseball, tennis, or lacrosse. It didn't really matter. As long as they were hanging out.

He continued his stroll across campus to the journalism school and kept going, past Florida Field, the football stadium, to the bat house. The bat house came down only four feet from the top, and the house was open at the bottom of the box. Like a shed way up off the ground — with no bottom, so the bats could fly in and out.

Chase stopped in front of the fence by the bat house and peered at it. It was quiet. Because it was morning, all of the bats were nestled inside, he figured. He knew they were waiting for the feeding time at dusk, when they would pour out — all 250,000 of them, he'd read — from the honeycomb of wooden ledges built up inside the enclosed space. The natural launch of bats each day resulted in a fifteen-minute frenzy of flight on their way to find insects to eat.

He was bored. No bats, no Tripp. He kept walking.

After a couple of minutes, Chase turned and walked across Museum Drive, walking down to the banks of Lake Alice. One of the central spots on campus, Lake Alice was home to the university's mascot: alligators. Live versions of the mascot anyway — it was *full* of alligators. Chase spent the next ten or fifteen minutes watching the alligators leisurely swim until they were on top of logs or the bank, even sometimes on top of each other warming their cold-blooded bodies in the midmorning sun. Chase headed back across campus toward his mom's office. He headed up the road next to the stadium, walking up to the gates. They were always open during the day, Chase knew, so anyone could enjoy the stadium. Maybe "enjoyed" was the wrong word because if it wasn't a game day, most people who used the stadium would walk or run up the eighty-five rows of bleachers in the heat and humidity, getting a workout for legs, hearts, and lungs.

Chase sat on the bleachers midway down to the field and opened the book he was carrying, *The Hobbit*, by JRR Tolkien. He tried to absorb the world Tolkien had created. He'd had trouble getting into it when it was first assigned. In fact, if it hadn't been required reading, Chase probably would have put it down for good after ten pages. Small human-like creatures with hair on the tops of their toes, plus elves and dwarves. It had sounded a little silly to him, but he soon found that he was lost, deep in Tolkien's Middle Earth.

Chase read for a while, helping Bilbo get through the Misty Mountains all the way to the Forest of Mirkwood, actually getting a lot of reading done.

Then he realized that he had no idea what he'd just read. His thoughts kept returning to Tripp. *Was he up yet? Was he sitting in the dark? Was everything better with his head?* Most importantly, *Was Tripp still mad?*

It was brutally hot so he took off his sweatshirt. He sat under the overhang in the south end zone of the stadium, staying in the shade, but still feeling the heat and humidity. He gave up trying to read once Bilbo arrived at Mirkwood. He might end up having to read all that part again. *Tripp.* Being on varsity hadn't turned out so great, after all.

Chase walked back to 2nd Avenue and his mom's office.

"Hey, Chase, you're back. Perfect." His mom straightened some papers on her desk and stood. "I was just finishing and am ready to go, if you are."

Chase nodded. "We headed to the mall?"

"Yes, let's go."

They drove west down University Avenue, Chase's third trip past the stadium of the day, out to Gainesville's Oaks Mall. They visited two sporting goods stores and Dillard's before Chase found a pair that were functional, cool, and not ridiculously high priced.

Chase didn't have much to say along the way, and his mom tried to talk for a while, eventually giving up. He could tell she was trying to take his mind off of Tripp.

"Let's make one more stop before we go. There's a new coffee shop in town that I want to try. I figured we might as well try it out now."

She pulled up in front of an old, beige Southern home on the north side of University Avenue as they were heading back toward campus. Chase read the sign as they got out of the car: "C-Y-Mplify."

"Pronounced like 'simplify'?" Chase asked.

"I think so," his mom answered. "It was opened recently by a couple of guys who've been in town for a long time. I went to a different high school than they did, but we actually knew each other in middle school."

They entered the shop, which had been a house before it was turned into a business. Chase wouldn't have been surprised to see someone walk out through one of the doors in pajamas. There was a long front porch they walked through to enter the building; a living room complete with couches, coffee table, and chairs; a dining room with a mirror and table; and the coffee prep area, with a barista today, which clearly had been someone's kitchen in a prior time. Chase's mom read the menu board for a moment, and ordered a Snickers latte.

"Chase, how about a hot chocolate?"

Chase thought.

"Okay, it's a special day. How about grape soda?"

"Sure!" said Chase. His mom didn't let him have soda often. Grape was his favorite, and they had lots and lots of flavors — all kinds of shapes and sizes of soda bottles — in the store.

"Hey, look who wandered in," a voice said behind them. They turned, and Chase saw a man of medium height and build, bald but looking otherwise close to his mom's forty-five years of age, along with a pretty woman with long, light brown hair.

"Ken Block! I brought Chase here for the first time, but didn't think we'd be so lucky to see you!" Chase hadn't heard his mom this excited since his last JV football game.

"Cindy, I'm so glad we're here today. It's always so good to see you," the man said.

"And Tracy," his mom said, "This is double the pleasure."

The woman smiled warmly, a smile that started at her mouth and worked its way to her deep brown eyes, two pools of caramel. His mom stepped forward to wrap each in a hug. She stepped back and the barista leaned forward, handing her the Snickers latte.

"Chase, let me introduce you."

"Hey, Chase, good to meet you," the man said, putting his hand out to shake Chase's. "I'm Ken Block."

The woman put out her hand to shake as well. "... And this is Tracy," chimed in his mom, completing the introductions. Both wore long-sleeved T-shirts and jeans and beamed at Chase. "We've known your mom since we were all young," said Ken, "which, as you can see" — he rubbed his hand over his shaved head — "has been longer for me then it was for your mom and Tracy."

They laughed and Chase joined in. He definitely seemed older. It was hard to picture them all as kids. "When she was little, your mom wanted to be a doctor and wanted to have kids. That's just about all she could ever talk about."

His mom laughed. "Well, I got part of it right. I have children, but I'm not a doctor."

Tracy smiled. "Cindy may have been the smartest person we've ever known."

Ken volunteered, "High school could've been a lot easier if she had been in all of our classes. Would've been nice to have had her help studying." Tracy nodded.

Chase spoke up, looking first at Ken with his black-framed, rectangular glasses, then at Tracy, "So, now you own a coffee shop?"

"Yes, Chase, we do. It's been a fun journey, trying to make a neat hangout place for the town."

"Chase, they named this place after one of Ken's

songs, 'Change Your Mind,' right, Ken?" Tracy and Ken nodded in response to Cindy's statement. "The 'C-Y-M' on this is an acronym from Change Your Mind."

"Cool," said Chase. "A coffee shop owner who writes songs." They all laughed, except for Chase. He could tell he was missing the shared joke. His mom patted him on the shoulder, while he tried not to feel embarrassed.

"Chase, I'm sorry. I guess I never mentioned Ken before. He's got a band called *Sister Hazel*. Having a coffee shop really isn't his main job; writing songs is."

Chase still didn't totally understand Ken's job, but it sounded pretty cool. "That's good," said Chase. "Do you know *Lecrae*?" Chase was thinking back to JB's pre-game music choice.

"No," Ken said. "I don't know *Lecrae*, but he's a great one. You know, a guy that I do know really well that you probably like is Darius Rucker. Great guy."

Tracy piped up. "We like *Sister Hazel*'s music too. You might like it as well." She grinned mischievously.

"I'm surprised your mom doesn't play it *all* the time," Ken said, and Chase could see that he was teasing his mom. Chase's mom blushed. "I'd guess we'd better listen to your stuff more often."

Chase's curiosity got the best of him. "So, you're like a songwriter and band manager?" That wasn't so hard to believe, Chase figured. Ken was kind of like a hip businessman with his cool T-shirt, funky glasses, and shaved head.

"No, Ken's a rock star," said his mom. When all the adults laughed, Chase was about to get flustered again when his mom quickly said, "No, *really* Chase. Seriously. We're just laughing because it still seems funny, even after all these years. He's the lead singer and they've had hit records. A true rock star."

"You certainly can't judge a book by its cover — at least if it's me," Ken laughed.

Chase nodded but stayed quiet, to not risk further embarrassment in this conversation — he'd never heard a *Sister Hazel* song. His mom and the Blocks chatted for a while longer, and then they headed back for Lincoln. Chase was quiet for a while watching the asphalt pass beneath their hood, and finally asked, "Really? He really plays in a band?"

"Absolutely. Just like I said — he's the lead singer, and writes most all their songs, I think."

"Cool," said Chase. "He doesn't exactly look the part, though."

His mom laughed. "He never has," she answered.

He hadn't anticipated meeting somebody famous today. All in all, he had to admit, it had been a fun day at UF with his mom.

And, it had helped take his mind off of last night, and Tripp.

At least for an afternoon.

CHAPTER 14

Tripp didn't come to school Monday. Chase hadn't seen him on Sunday, either. Neither was a total surprise. He'd been by the house twice Sunday afternoon to check, and had spoken with Tripp's mom and sister again. They said Tripp should be back to school soon.

It was making Chase's stomach hurt, and he was glad that Coach Skalaski held short practices on Mondays. It was a day to watch film, catch up on schoolwork and science labs, and stretch out the soreness. He was glad JV was over.

As soon as he finished practice Monday afternoon, Chase's mom drove him north up Highway 301 from Lincoln to Interstate 10 and east into Jacksonville. They didn't talk much; she knew that the stuff with Tripp was weighing heavily on his mind, and there wasn't much left to say.

His mom started to park her Toyota Tundra in a spot outside the stadium, when Chase pointed toward the entrance gate. "You can just drop me off," he said. "I can get myself in, and you can head off to the mall." Chase's mom didn't mind occasionally driving him to Jacksonville, as it gave her a chance to go over to the new St. John's Town Place Center and its acres of outdoor shopping and nice stores, none of which could be found in Lincoln.

"You sure?" she asked.

"I'm sure, I've done this a million times."

Chase walked through the short concrete poles and planters that ringed the stadium, the City of Jacksonville's attempt to keep a truck bomb or anyone else with bad intentions away from Sunday afternoon football crowds. He touched the shoulder of the big obsidian sailor statue, which stood two feet taller than he, as he walked past.

A sailor from a Navy destroyer.

He buzzed at the gate, thankful that the weather was cooling and the concrete wasn't hot anymore. He didn't have to wait long. The guard, Tony, recognized him and buzzed him through the gate quickly.

"Coming for Mr. Stevens?"

Chase nodded and Tony walked him back through the maze of cubicles and offices in the Destroyers' ticketing and public relations departments to the main hallway running underneath the stadium.

Shawn Stevens' name was on the wall outside a small office on the other side of the hallway, tucked in next to the visitors' locker room, a few steps away from the coaches' offices. As Chase expected, Mr. Stevens was in his office watching film, but he was surprised to see that there was another man seated across his desk in the darkened office. Chase paused in the doorway.

"Come on in, Chase. Coach Douglas and I are watching last week's game between the Carolina Tigers and the Atlanta Redhawks. We'll be done in a few minutes, but you may as well watch with us now."

Mr. Stevens explained, as he ran the game film back and forth, back and forth, back and forth. They were watching a running back that the Carolina Tigers had just released. "We liked this guy when he was coming out of Notre Dame, but the Tigers drafted him. It's only been two years, and he never did much for them. They didn't play him much, and he hardly ever carried the ball. We're trying to see if he's worth putting on our roster."

Coach Douglas never took his eyes off the screen. "Watch how he drops his hips. Love his change of direction. I don't see how they think Tate is better than this kid, but I'm glad they do."

Mr. Stevens spoke. "So you like him better than Bullitt? You think he makes us better in the backfield?"

"Definitely. Not even close. I'll go tell Coach Kushner and see what he thinks. You wanna go talk to Christian?" Christian Flaherty, Chase knew, was the

Destroyers' General Manager and Mr. Stevens' boss. He and Keith Kushner, the head coach, made the final decisions on who should be on the roster. They really listened to what Mr. Stevens thought, though. He had picked a great number of the players on the roster.

"Chase, I need you to give me a minute, and let me go talk to some folks. You know where the fridge is, and here — let me put in last week's tape and you can watch Owen." Chase knew that professional football no longer used videotape or any other kind of tape, or even film, even though everyone still used both terms. It was all digital now. Mr. Stevens merely clicked his mouse a couple of times to pull up the Destroyers' win of the day before over the New York Fighters.

"Go to the second quarter. He made some great decisions, and his footwork was really good, including some great play action throws."

Mr. Stevens headed off down the hall, and Chase followed him for the first few steps to the large, clear-windowed refrigerator, full of plastic bottles of Gatorade and water. He grabbed a Gatorade, purple, of course, and headed back to the dark office.

Tripp's dad returned about twenty minutes later.

"Sorry about that. Thanks for waiting." Chase nodded. "We're gonna claim him; don't know if we'll get him."

"Why don't you know? Aren't you just trading for him with Carolina?" Chase asked.

"No," Mr. Stevens said. "Carolina has already taken him off their roster, so any team can tell the NFL Office in New York that they want to 'claim' him. We just sent that in. If we're the only team that does by the 4:00 deadline, then we get him. If there is more than one, then the League gives him to the worst team."

"So they can get better."

"Right," Mr. Stevens said. "So we won't know if we get him until later tonight." Chase nodded again.

Mr. Stevens turned even more serious. "I was going to come home this weekend when I heard about Tripp's injury. I hated that I wasn't there, but then Tripp's mom told me that the doctors said Tripp just needed to sleep this weekend. The only thing is … that he knows that he's probably done for the year, I think. More than just sitting out the next two games. He won't even speak. I can't tell if he's tired or angry. Or both." The dark blue eyes looked troubled. Mr. Stevens ran a hand through his blond hair.

"Do you mind telling me what happened Friday night? I've heard it from Todd, Coach Skalaski, and the doctors, but you were right there."

Chase told the story from the beginning. He tried to start with the hit but Tripp's dad made him back up and tell him everything he could remember about that entire night. About the bus ride, what warmups were like, about the fans at Bartram, everything leading up to the hit. Anything that might help him understand what was going on.

"Why do you want to know all that?" Chase asked.

"I don't know," Mr. Stevens said. "I'm sure it won't help, but I just want to hear everything as best as I can."

Chase began telling Mr. Stevens everything he could remember. Mr. Stevens interrupted once or twice with questions about details, but mostly sat quiet, listening. Chase finally reached the hit and thinking Tripp wasn't breathing.

"Wow. That was pretty scary, I'll bet," said Mr. Stevens.

Chase nodded. "I was scared." He hadn't told anyone that he thought Tripp was dead. He'd just said, "not breathing," before but never really admitted he thought Tripp was dead. He'd felt silly earlier, but when he started telling everything to Mr. Stevens the emotion of the story came pouring out, including thinking Tripp was dead. He told Tripp's dad that Tripp even questioned why Chase was on the sidelines.

Tripp's dad shook his head.

"You did the right thing. Tripp would've done the same for you. Well, I hope he would have." He sighed. "Telling the truth is always the right thing. I'm sure Tripp knows that. We just need to figure out what's going on with him.

"There's probably no point in checking in again for a couple of days. We take him to the doctor on Friday, and you have a game that night at Union County. Why don't you come by Saturday morning? It should all be back to normal. I think."

Chase nodded. He hoped Mr. Stevens was right.

He left the office and found his mom waiting outside. He didn't much want to talk about it, but found himself telling her about their talk. Before he could finish, his phone buzzed with a text message.

"We got him! Our claim went through and we got him from Carolina!!!!!!!"

Chase smiled. He figured the Destroyers offices would be a happy place tonight. He was glad someone would be happy.

CHAPTER 15

Chase walked in the house after practice on Tuesday, eating gummy bears that he'd gotten at a convenience store on his way home. He was pleasantly surprised to find Granny and Gramps at the house. His mother's parents lived in South Jacksonville now, near Bartram Trail and not too far from Lincoln, and occasionally came over for visits.

"Thought we'd stop in and see our favorite daughter and our wonderful grandchildren," Gramps said.

"I'm your *only* daughter," Mom said, dryly.

"Who's counting?" Gramps said. "Now come over here, Chase, and give your favorite grandfather a proper hug." Technically, Gramps *was* his favorite grandfather and everyone knew it. Dad's father died in a car accident before Chase was born, so he never met the man.

"Stop it, George," Granny said.

She tilted her head and pointed at her left cheek. Chase smiled and planted a kiss on that exact spot. Thinking about his father made Chase automatically glance at Mom. He was struck at how young she seemed. *She had to think about Dad sometimes too, right?*

"We went over to Gainesville, where your granddad had a doctor's appointment." Gramps had been fighting cancer for the last year, and while he still looked healthy and fine on the outside, Chase could tell that his mom was worried about her dad.

"Why did he go over there?" Most of Gramps' doctor visits had been at the Mayo clinic in Jacksonville.

"He's maybe going to try a different treatment. Something that some researchers in Gainesville have come up with, that might knock this thing out a little quicker," said Granny. Chase suspected that it wasn't an issue with the speed of the cure, but rather whether there was *any* cure at all for Gramps. Hopefully he was wrong, but he wondered if the experimental treatment was a last ditch effort. He hoped not, and pushed the thought out of his mind.

"I hear that you've been playing on the varsity this year. That is fantastic. We are so proud of you," said his grandfather.

"We sure are," said Granny.

They used to attend games, but with his health, they didn't go to many anymore.

His grandfather continued to talk, and shook his head

when Chase remembered that he was still holding the bag of gummy bears and offered them to the others.

"No, thanks. You know, the team really looks good this year. Even better than last year's team. In fact, this is one of the best 4A teams I've *ever* seen from Carr or anywhere, and I've seen a lot of them." The 4A classification was for schools with under one thousand students, and Carr had already clinched their district title in the 4A classification, and was assured of a playoff berth. Raines had clinched a berth also, and was also 4A. They would probably have to deal with the Vikings again later if they hoped to win a state championship.

"Thank you. I'm really, really, really excited," Chase said. He blushed slightly. "We're really good, but I'm not getting to play very much. But I am really excited to be on varsity. I didn't even know if it was allowed, but I didn't want to ask and maybe mess it up."

Gramps laughed. "Of course you didn't! But, no, it's certainly allowed. Since your school has all grades at one school, every student can play every sport, at any level. But even if you don't play much, you know as well as I do that there are lots of ways to help the team. Plus, it's not like Coach is just trying to do you a favor. He wouldn't have you on varsity if he didn't *want* you there."

Chase nodded.

Gramps continued, "They wouldn't be bringing you up if they didn't think you were going to help them in some way. Coach Skalaski doesn't mess around. Everything he does, he does for a reason, because he's thought about it."

The noise brought Hannah out of her room, followed by Megan.

"What are you doing here?" Hannah asked.

"Just visiting the doctor," Granny said.

"And congratulating Chase," Gramps said. "An eighth-grader on the varsity team is rare. Even in a small school."

"Uh, I'm on varsity," Megan said.

"Yes," Gramps said, "I am in no way surprised, knowing your father and JB."

"Let's celebrate over dinner," Mom said, "before my spaghetti congeals!"

Chase spoke up during dinner. "Even if I don't get to play very much, I'd be happy just to be part of the team."

"Even if you don't play much, there are lots of ways to help," Megan said.

"Skalaski wouldn't ask you to be on varsity if he didn't think you were capable," Gramps said.

"How do you know so much about Coach?" Megan asked.

"Back in the day, I was a linebacker when Carr was still River City High. But trust me, the entire Carr football program can thank Coach Skalaski for where it is today."

No one spoke for the next few minutes, digesting this information, along with their dinner. The only sound came from the scraping of forks on plates until Megan asked, "Was Union County still our rival back then?"

Gramps put his fork down and wiped his stubbly chin with his napkin. Chase could see he was thinking about it, remembering. "When Coach Skalaski took over, Carr had lost eighteen of the last twenty games against the Union County Tigers, and the Tigers reeled off six straight more wins, but then the tide shifted."

Mom was clearing dishes by now, and Megan jumped up to help. "Thank you so much, Megan, but I've got it under control," Mom said.

"I'll help," Hannah said. "I'll let those who live and breathe football stay to hear the story."

"I didn't know some of this," Chase said.

"I didn't know *any* of this," Megan said. "Please, continue."

"In his first few years, Coach Skalaski told the players that the Union game was no big deal. He wanted his players to focus on improving skills. But Carr was suddenly winning district games, and soon enough we had a chance at actually beating the Union County Tigers. Well, how the Loggerheads perform against the Tigers is a good measuring stick of just how much Carr has improved on the gridiron."

"But, Gramps," Chase said, "Union is our rival. It's *the* rival. We *have* to beat them!"

Gramps shook his head and smiled. "No you don't. It might seem like an important game because Union is your rival and because you know their players from Little League, but you don't need to win this game. It really doesn't matter."

"No way!" said Megan, looking like she was ready to burst out of her chair.

Gramps laughed. "That's right. Even when we try to say it doesn't matter who wins, you guys know better — it does."

This year was no different. Carr had lost its last two games, both non-district games against Raines and Bartram Trail, but was back at full strength for the Union County game. Union County, meanwhile, was ranked number two in 1A and was sitting with a 9 – 0 record.

All three of these games didn't matter to Carr's playoff hopes, and the players knew it. At the same time, they still wanted to win.

Chase could tell from practice that week that Coach Skalaski didn't want to enter the playoffs on a three-game losing streak, either.

After dinner, his grandparents visited for another thirty minutes or so, before heading off to their home in St. Johns County over near the beach. He was glad to see them and enjoyed talking to Gramps about the game.

Chase turned on the TV and fell into the sofa. He'd just shut his eyes when he heard, "So what exactly happens in a concussion?" *Wha — ?*

Chase shot to an upright position. It was an episode of *MythBusters* on Discovery Channel, and a "bashed-brain expert" was now talking: "A concussion is when you transfer a force, external, through the skull to the brain. Think of the skull as a box, and you've got the brain inside which is the consistency of Jell-O." Chase was glued. *You had me at Jell-O*, he thought to himself as he watched one of the show's hosts make a gelatin brain mold.

Dr. Brain Bash continued, "When a concussion occurs and forces delivery to the skull itself, the skull moves relative to the brain — the brain stays in one place, the skull moves against it. That can bruise the brain that's hitting the skull and it can actually damage the brain opposite that." It all sounded so clinical.

"It's all a function of force. It's how much energy is transmitted to the skull and to the brain that determines how severe the concussion is or how much injury there is to the brain."

"It sounds like the bottom line is whatever kind of blow moves the head more violently is what's gonna cause more of a concussion, right?" said a host. They were testing the potential damage to brains by bottle-breaking, like you see in bar-brawl scenes in Wild West movies.

"Even though after a few beers it might seem like a good idea to hit somebody over the head with a beer bottle, it's probably not. Nevertheless, we feel inclined to get up close and personal on our testing and that's where this comes in," said the host as he raised a football helmet into full view. "This is a football helmet outfitted with a specially designed array of accelerometers that will register any movement of our skull and help us determine whether a full vs. empty beer bottle is more harmful." They put the helmet on a mannequin head and tried to break bottles over it.

I swear this has to be a sign from God, Chase pondered. He imagined Tripp's head being banged around inside the helmet. He felt queasy. And then ... a wave of relief. Now he *knew* he'd done the right thing in being truthful on the field about Tripp's injury.

Even though parts of it felt like he'd betrayed his friend — there was that look during the game in Tripp's eyes that pleaded, *Have my back, bro* — deep down, Chase was certain he totally *had* backed his best bud. Chase was glad he'd found the courage to follow his own gut.

Tripp might be mad, but he'll get over it ... eventually.

Chase texted Tripp hey, but Tripp never responded to Chase's text that night.

CHAPTER 16

Chase finished his barbecue sandwich and got up, done with pregame meal. JB looked up at him.

"I thought you were making progress," the outsized quarterback said. No vest today. He was wearing a mostly red checked flannel shirt with jeans, and looked more like a big farmer — farmer strong! — than a star quarterback. "You'd actually been eating pregame meals these days. I've noticed. You must be calmer. Except now …" He grinned that grin of his and pointed at Chase's plate. The sandwich was half-eaten.

Chase smiled. "I don't suppose I need to go yet. I can hang out longer before I go get dressed and try to eat some more." They were sitting in the cafeteria, and would need to be on the bus, dressed and ready to go to Lake Butler shortly.

"So why aren't you eating? Again. Do we need to

send you to a doctor?" JB smiled, but he looked a little serious too.

"No, I'm okay." Chase paused. "But *Tripp* went to the doctor today."

"What'd the doctor say?"

"Well, up to today, he's been having to stay in the dark and, well, um – "

"Yes, I know," JB cut in. He could tell Chase felt awkward. "Megan has been giving me updates from Hannah."

"Oh, *great*," Chase said and frowned.

"It's okay. Hannah just cares about you. And about Tripp. Megan does too. Sounds like you're ready to start talking with him again, hanging out." JB smiled, but it wasn't the usual big smile. It was gentler, softer. Chase nodded but didn't say anything. He was afraid his voice would crack because he was about to cry.

"So, you haven't heard what the doctor said today?"

Chase shook his head no, then took a deep breath. "No, his dad said I should come by tomorrow."

"That sounds right," said JB. "You'll get it figured out."

"I hope so." Chase looked down at his sandwich. Now he was sure he couldn't eat another bite. He stood. "You want me to wait, JB?"

"No, no, go ahead. I'll be right behind you," said the quarterback.

Chase walked down the tile hallway away from the

cafeteria until he reached the end of the main building, exiting the door and walking across the courtyard
to the sidewalk that led to the gym behind the school.

He got dressed, moving slowly. He preferred to get
into the locker room early but then take his time. Don't
rush.

Eventually the locker room filled up and he could
feel it in the air around him. It was almost like static
electricity, you could feel the buzzing, right at the sur-
face. He wasn't entirely sure why, but he truly enjoyed
being around the guys and soaking up the anticipation
of the game.

Knowing that they would be on the field shortly,
the unknown of how they would each play. And then,
would their play add up to a win? His nerves were on
high alert. No JV game, so he would finally play for the
varsity, Coach said. He wouldn't play much, but even
his few times playing on the kickoff team could make
a difference if he could help make a tackle.

Every now and then, but not very often, thank
goodness, the thought *would I get hurt* crossed Chase's
mind. He figured it crossed everyone's mind, especially
since most everyone would play even more than he
did. But nobody talked about it.

Of course, he knew that it had been on his mind a
lot lately because of Tripp's injury. Not as much out of
worry but because he just wanted to see Tripp. Things
had just gotten good with both of them on varsity.

But now ... Chase felt bad for Tripp. He also felt bad for himself.

Maybe it would all change tomorrow.

The bus ride to Lake Butler was quick. Straight out of Lincoln, fourteen miles west on Highway 100, then a left on 6th Street as they reached town, then around to Union County High School.

It was still an hour and a half until kickoff, yet the stands were already filling. That didn't usually happen. Chase thought football games in Lincoln were a pretty big deal, but based on how many people were already in the stands and hanging around as the bus pulled up, he saw that it was even bigger in Lake Butler. Or at least the people of Lake Butler thought the Carr game was bigger.

When they came off the field following pre-game warmups, a hand grabbed Chase's left arm around his bicep. He turned, startled, and saw a serious-looking JB holding him with his huge right hand. "Come with me," JB said, and led him past the locker room door to the back of the building. His voice sounded low and grim.

The stands were still filling and there were people everywhere, except where JB led. It was dark, and quiet, as if they'd left the field miles behind. "What are you doing?" Chase asked.

JB smiled. "Sorry that I didn't think of this earlier." He grew serious again. "Do you mind if we pray?"

"Uh, no. I guess not. Here?"

"Sure, this works fine. We're just talking to God. This spot will work."

"Do we have time?" Their teammates would be checking their equipment and tape and getting ready to take the field in a few minutes.

"Depends how long I'm gonna pray, now, doesn't it?" JB laughed. Chase wasn't sure if he was kidding. "Relax, buddy," said JB.

JB put his hand on Chase's shoulder pad and began to pray. He prayed for safety for both teams, for safe travels for the fans, and for Tripp and his family. That Tripp would heal, and that he would return to normal. Soon. And he prayed for faith and calm for Chase.

"Amen," said JB. Chase opened his eyes and looked at JB. He was surprised how much better he felt. "All right, Chase. You've delayed us long enough. We'd better get in the locker room," said JB, and laughed.

By the time they took the sideline for kickoff, Chase saw that not only were the *stands* on both sides packed, but the fence circling the track around the field had people standing two or three deep all the way around.

This was far larger than the Bartram Trail crowd, which was the biggest he'd seen.

Megan kicked off to start the game. With JV ending the week before, Chase was playing on the kickoff and punt teams. Not much, but enough to be exciting.

He streaked down the field on the left side, trying to avoid the purple jerseys coming at him. It didn't work, and he ran straight into a guy, number fifty-five, and was knocked to the ground.

He never saw the Union County kick returner catch the ball at his own 8-yard line, fake as if he was going to run to his left, and then head back toward his right, across the field, and then cut through a gap to the sideline. He streaked up the sideline in his purple jersey with a white number twenty and gold stripe on the sleeves, white pants with purple stripes, and gold helmet with a purple UCH and tiger head on each side.

Meanwhile, there didn't seem to be any of Carr's players in their white jerseys, blue numbers and helmets, and blue pants with green stripes, anywhere near him. Finally, around the 50-yard line, Megan Brown was the only Carr player between number twenty and the end zone. She was the "safety" for the play because she was the kicker, staying farther back than the others. By now Chase had scrambled to his feet and was running to catch up. He held his breath — Megan was tall and a great kicker, but she was only an eighth-grader about to tackle this kid near the sideline ... Number twenty cut back toward the middle of the field, making Megan miss as she went past him, but her effort slowed him and allowed another of Carr's players to catch up with the returner, finally tackling him at the Carr 10-yard line.

The Lake Butler crowd was going wild.

Stay together.

Coach Skalaski's last words before they exited the locker room were to "Stay together. We may have adversity tonight — they are really good. And they're fast. In fact, we are sure to have adversity at some point tonight. It may come early or it may come later. The one thing I can promise you is that at some point tonight, things will be bad. Like life sometimes."

Stay together.

Turns out things were going to be bad early in the game. Union County scored a touchdown on the next play.

7 – 0, Union County, only twenty seconds into the game.

The game was a barnburner from there. JB led the Loggerheads down the field for a tying touchdown, then, after each team punted, Union County scored another touchdown.

14 – 7, UCH.

The Browns combined to add to the score for Carr, as JB led the offense down the field until the drive stalled, and Megan kicked a 32-yard field goal.

14 – 10, Union County.

Chase ran down on the kickoffs each time Carr scored, but he didn't make any tackles. Fortunately, other guys were and there'd be no more returns to Carr's 10-yard line. After Megan's kickoff, the Tigers got the ball and were forced to punt. Defense was getting it done! Three plays later JB scored on a 50-yard run.

17 — 14, Carr was finally ahead!

That was the halftime score, and the Carr faithful cheered as loud as they could as the players headed to the locker room.

The second half was more of the same. The teams exchanged touchdowns, and then Megan added another field goal. It was now 27 — 21 Carr, with five minutes left in the game.

Chase had played on seven plays, on both Carr's punts as well as Union County's. He'd had an uneventful night as a player but a thrilling run as a spectator. He thought of Tripp when Jackson Parker, who had replaced Tripp, caught a touchdown pass. But he realized that he hadn't *worried* about Tripp once since he'd gone behind the locker room with JB.

Now Carr's defense just needed to hang on, something that both teams had difficulty with this night.

The crowd roared — and Chase groaned — as Union County relentlessly drove down the field for the go-ahead touchdown, scoring with a minute and five seconds left in the game. The Union County kicker made the extra point, and Carr found itself trailing 28 — 27 with sixty-five seconds left.

Chase overheard as JB rallied the offense to take the field one last time.

"It's been a long night, guys. We're tired, they're tired. Even young men will stumble and fall. But those who wait upon the Lord will renew their strength." JB's voice was booming now, in the middle of the eager offensive players. "They will rise up on wings like eagles. Those that wait upon the Lord will renew their strength. They will walk and not grow tired; they will run and not be faint.

"That is *us*. We've got sixty-five seconds left. *Let's go score!*"

Coach Skalaski walked over and put his hand on JB's shoulder. "We're going to win this," Coach said.

JB nodded, his eyes flashing.

"We just went over that, Coach." He grinned.

Coach Skalaski nodded, not sure what JB was talking about, but not doubting him. "Don't forget that a field goal wins it. That's all we need, and Megan has a strong leg. You need to use our time wisely and get the ball down around their 20-yard line." A field goal with the ball on the 20-yard line would be a 37-yard field goal.

Megan had made longer this year, but Coach wanted her to feel as comfortable as possible with the distance and the kick. Making it harder, Carr was headed toward the north end zone in this fourth and final quarter, and there was a slight breeze coming at them. The wind would be in Megan's face, so Coach didn't want her worrying about a long kick into the wind. Nice and short. JB nodded again, then took the field with the offense after the kickoff, starting from Carr's own 30-yard line.

A quick pass to Dimitri, who got out of bounds and

stopped the clock with fifty seconds left, put the ball on the Carr 45-yard line. Carr only needed thirty-five more yards to get down to Union County's 20-yard line.

The next play, JB ran *Solo Right 12 Read,* a play that was a quarterback option run. JB was responsible for the "Read" portion of the play, because he had to "read the defense" and decide whether to keep the ball and run himself or give it to Scott MacLean, the tailback.

JB caught the shotgun snap with two receivers split out to the right, and one split to the left, with his tailback, Scott, standing to his left. The "read" for JB was simple but had to be done quickly. He needed to decide if the left defensive end was a threat, because the play left that end as the lone unblocked defender. Otherwise, he would keep the ball and run it himself.

The left end rushed hard and crashed down toward the ball. JB read it correctly in the split second he had to decide. JB faked a handoff to Scott and kept the ball, running past the end who could not adjust in time and turned his head as JB ran past, then JB ran behind a beautiful block from Jackson and Dimitri, the receivers. He crossed the 50, then the 40, the 30, and the 20, and was finally knocked out of bounds at the 10-yard line. First down, and the clock had stopped with thirty-five seconds left.

Best yet, Carr hadn't used its only remaining time-out. Coach Skalaski signaled to JB. The referee placed the ball on the left hashmark, since JB had run out of bounds on the left side of the field. It was a short field goal — only twenty-seven yards.

In some ways, that actually made the kick more difficult because it made the angle more extreme from the hashmark. Chase had heard Megan explain to Hannah that it seems backwards, but sometimes a team can be *too* close, because the kicker's angle gets too sharp. A little farther back can make it more in the middle, a little straighter.

JB got Coach's signal, and took the snap from the center. He ran several steps to his right until he was almost exactly in the middle of the field, and fell down. JB hopped up, handed the ball to the official, and said a few words to him. Both the official and JB then turned toward the clock, just standing there, while the crowd stood up and watched the clock tick down.

Twenty-one, twenty, nineteen, eighteen. The clock was ticking, and the crowd fell silent.

JB glanced toward the sideline, and Coach Skalaski flashed the number five, spreading all his fingers and holding it out toward JB with an open palm. JB turned back toward the clock, standing next to the official. They kept watching.

The clock kept counting down: ten ... nine ... eight ... seven ... six ... JB turned toward the official and said something. The official blew his whistle, raising his arms over his head.

"Time-out, Carr! Their third and final timeout!"

Five seconds left. Coach Skalaski had wanted five seconds left when Megan tried the game-winning field goal.

JB trotted off the field, as his sister trotted on. He had lost three yards by running to the side and back on the play, so that the ball was now on the 13-yard line. It was well worth the trade-off, because a thirty-yard kick from the middle of the field would be much easier than an angled twenty-seven yard attempt.

By letting the clock run down to five seconds, Chase realized that Coach Skalaski had ensured that Carr would win or lose the game on Megan's kick. By the time the ball was snapped, placed down, kicked, and then landed, more than five seconds would have gone by. There would be no time for any further plays by Union County if the kick was good — or by Carr if she missed.

Chase stood by JB. Both had their helmets off, standing on the sidelines, watching. JB began quickly walking backwards down the sideline, away from the goalposts. "Where you going?" Chase murmured.

"Back here. Better angle to watch the kick." Moving farther away from the kick down the sideline gave JB and Chase a slightly better view from their position on whether the ball was going through the uprights or not. Of course, the official would tell them soon enough with his signal anyway.

And the crowd.

Mr. Stevens had told Chase and Tripp that the quickest way to tell if the kick was good was *not* by watching the ball, but by watching *fans* in the end zone who had a clear, straight-on view of the ball coming at them.

Tripp. In the excitement, Chase thought of Tripp again. He was ready for good news tomorrow morning.

And tonight, from Megan's foot.

The entire stadium was on its feet, most everyone in purple and yellow, but the outnumbered loyal Loggerhead fans stayed silent but hopeful. The Union County fans weren't silent. They were making as much noise as they could, in hopes of distracting Megan.

"She's got to be nervous," said Chase.

"Yes, she is," said JB, "but she does a really nice job of breathing deep, staying calm, and she repeats the 23rd Psalm over and over."

"Isn't that long? The whole thing?"

JB's grin was not as wide and bright as usual, but showed the tension of the moment. "No, not the whole thing. She just murmurs, 'The Lord is my shepherd, the Lord is my shepherd, the Lord is my shepherd' and she says everything gets cleared out of her head. All the negativity, everything. Dad suggested it to her last year."

Just then, Will Kingston snapped the ball. Roger Dalton, who was also the holder, took the snap and placed it down. So far, so good. Megan connected and the ball took off, airborne. Almost right away, the ball started spinning crazy and stopped going up, but started flying flatter to the ground. A Union County rusher had gotten his hand on Megan's kick.

Blocked!

Megan's kick was blocked by a jumping Tiger defender!

But Megan had kicked it so hard that the ball continued forward through the air, even though it was spinning strangely and was no longer headed up. The ball hit the crossbar, the parallel bar at the bottom of the uprights, which the kick has to clear to be good. It bounced off the crossbar, and continued forward, rising over the crossbar and falling ... just over it.

The referee raised both arms straight up over his head. The kick was good!

Carr won, 30 — 28!

JB and Chase hugged, then JB and the rest of the team started running out toward his sister.

The majority of the stadium was silent, but the Carr fans were making plenty of noise.

CHAPTER 17

Chase didn't sleep well that night. When he got home, he was still amped about the win over Lake Butler. And then, as that faded, he grew worried about seeing Tripp the next morning. He knew everything should be fine, but he was still worried about Tripp's head ... and his reaction to Chase.

At 8:00 am on Saturday, he walked next door. He'd been sitting around since 6:00 am, waiting for a decent hour to arrive. Mrs. Stevens came to the door.

"Good morning, Chase," she said. "I'm afraid Tripp isn't up yet." Chase's face fell.

"Okay. I'll stop back by." He turned to go, then stopped. "What did the doctor say?"

"It was mixed. He can go back to school, but can't play football yet. The doctor said that the brain is like a muscle. Tripp needs to exercise it but when it gets sore — or since it's the brain, when he gets a head-ache — he needs to stop using it."

"That sounds hard. But kind of good, I guess. How was he with the news?" Chase asked.

"Not very happy. He can't wait to get back to foot-ball, especially now that the playoffs are here." After the game last night, Carr learned their first-round opponent in the Florida High School 4A playoffs would be the Eastside Rams of Gainesville. It would be a short trip next Friday. Apparently Tripp wouldn't make it, at least not in uniform.

"I understand. That would be hard." She nodded as he spoke. "Well, I'll come back later."

Chase stopped back at 10:00 am, and Mrs. Stevens opened the door. "You can go on back," she said. Chase smiled, but it was a tight smile. He was nervous and it showed. "He seems to be doing well," she said. "He's in much better spirits than he was yesterday."

Chase walked down the hall to Tripp's room and found the door slightly open. "Hey, Tripp." He tried to sound light and cheery.

Tripp looked up and saw Chase.

"Hey."

Chase couldn't read Tripp's expression.

"Your mom told me that you can head back to school."

"Yep."

Chase waited, but Tripp didn't say anything else. Awkward. Not a good sign. He wasn't sure what to say.

Chase finally broke the silence. "Megan had an amazing game last night. Coach gave her another game ball — her second of the year! She made a field goal on the last play and ..."

"Yeah, I know. Look, no offense, but maybe you don't need to come by here anymore. You don't need to keep acting like we're friends. Or, did you come here to see my *dad*?"

Chase stepped back toward Tripp's bedroom door, feeling like he'd been punched in the gut.

"Don't bother."

Chase was floored. It was the worst thing he could have thought of — worse, really. He felt like he'd been punched.

He tried once more.

"See ya, Thug ..."

Tripp snorted. "Just close the door when you go."

Chase walked out in a daze, and headed toward the front door. On his way out, he heard Tripp's mom call out from the kitchen.

"How did it go?"

"Fine," he tried to call out. Instead, his voice came out in a squeak. Of course it did — that's how his day was going.

Chase staggered through his classes the next few days. He was having trouble focusing, between feeling awful about his friendship with Tripp and all the excitement of the upcoming playoff game, it was no wonder. Tripp was back at school, which only seemed to make matters worse. He was sitting several seats away from Chase in each class they had together. Worse yet, Tripp sat next to Kate in algebra both days. Chase figured he did it just to annoy him.

Wednesday morning, Chase saw Hannah and Kate as he was walking out of the auditorium with some of the other players. "What'd you think?" he asked.

"I thought she was great," said Hannah, and Kate nodded in agreement.

The "she" they were talking about was Mo Isom, an All Southeastern Conference soccer player who had just graduated from Louisiana State University. After finishing her soccer career, she had tried out for the LSU football team as a kicker.

Carr had held a special Wednesday assembly at which Mo spoke to the students about hopes, dreams, and going to class. Not necessarily in that order.

"Totally," said Chase.

"And I think she's coming out to talk to the football team tonight," said Megan. Chase hadn't seen her, but Megan walked up, apparently having been seated in the auditorium with Kate and Hannah. Lately, Megan and Hannah included Kate more too. Chase was pretty pleased about that, especially since Tripp was sitting with her and ignoring him. Anything that made it more likely that he could see Kate on a regular basis.

"Oh, that'll be cool. I could listen to her all day," Chris Kingston said.

"You know what I thought was cool," said Megan. "She's six feet tall and said that she weighs like 195 pounds."

"And she's beautiful," chimed in Will Kingston, who had walked up. Everyone nodded.

"Sometimes the magazines are wrong," Kate said. "There's more to life than being really skinny."

Others nodded and they started to head toward their next class. Chase saw Tripp walk by out of the corner of his eye. Tripp didn't stop.

Practice was nearing an end. Chase hadn't done much other than playing on the Scout Team, where he was running the offense and simulating Keith Ware, Eastside's star quarterback. Doing a good job on Scout Team *did* help the defense, he knew. And he knew that someday he'd have a chance to play more in games. He just needed to be patient.

Running plays on the Scout Team wasn't glamorous, but most everyone had done it at some point in their football lives. It was a necessary part of being a team player, and something of a rite of passage — something you had to go through. Even JB, who had been the starting quarterback ever since he arrived as a home-school walk-on to the Carr team in ninth grade, had volunteered to help on the Scout Team from time to time. The coaches had always been really clear about that way of helping the team. Chase took it seriously, running hard in practice through the opponent's plays, learning as many of them as he could from memory, to try and help the defense prepare.

Toward the end of practice, Coach Skalaski told Chase to go in for Roger Dalton, the backup quarterback, and run a couple of plays, his reward for running Scout Team so enthusiastically. Chase went in and ran a couple of plays, handing off to a running back each time, running *Right 24 Power* and the *Left 23 Power*, two of Carr's basic bread-and-butter running plays. Chase knew that if somehow anything happened to JB and Roger, his job would simply be to hand off to the running backs until one of them could get back into the game.

After those two plays, Coach blew his whistle and sent everyone in to the Team Meeting Room.

Some players sat in chairs or on desks, while others stood around the perimeter. Soon, the room was packed with damp boys in soggy uniforms, most of them glad to be in dry shelter. Chase and JB stood in back. Megan looked at them from the front and gave an excited thumbs-up. She was jumping up and down. In a moment, the boys knew why.

Despite Coach Skalaski's lanky build, he commanded the room. "We've invited a great athlete to come and speak to you today. She's a record-breaking soccer player, a recent graduate of Louisiana State University. It's an honor for us to introduce Mo Isom."

Megan was giggling like a ... well, an eighth-grader. She was a big fan since she'd read about how Mo had trained to kick for LSU's football team. "I'm so excited to hear you talk, and I want you to know how much you've inspired me ..."

"Okay, Megan," Coach Skalaski said. Everyone laughed. "Let us hear what Mo has to say."

"Yeah, but just one more thing ... "

Apparently, Megan couldn't help herself. Chase could see her blushing through her milk-chocolate skin. He looked away quickly to avoid cracking up.

"I'm an eighth-grader," Megan sputtered, "but I play kicker for the varsity team. There. Just had to say."

"That's amazing," Mo smiled. "Thank you for sharing." She turned toward everyone. "I'm so glad to be here today. We don't have much time so I thought we could have a little Q-and-A session. Ask me anything." Of course, Megan's hand shot up first. "Yes, go ahead," Mo said.

"What is it about you that makes you so *good* at everything you do, like, against the odds?" Megan asked. "What's your secret to success?"

Mo giggled. "No secret. It's very simple: Discover who God made you to be, and you'll discover success. Don't sell yourself short. Don't sell yourself out."

Chase liked how Mo was to-the-point and decided to raise his hand. Mo pointed to him, and Chase wished he could get a do-over but it was too late — all eyes were on him. "Well, I love football," Chase said, quietly but audibly, "but sometimes I feel like I'm never getting anywhere with it. So how do you excel?"

Mo nodded, an understanding nod. She was tall but not intimidating. *She's pretty.* Chase was not the only boy in the room thinking that.

"Contentment is a state of mind and heart, not status," Mo said, making direct eye contact with Chase. "If you're chasing a spot on varsity because you think sports will make you happy, give it a rest. Find gratitude and pure happiness in exactly where you are and who you are and what you already have."

After she answered several questions from other players, Coach Skalaski stood next to Megan and addressed the group. "Okay, we only have time for one more question with Mo."

JB raised his hand for the last one. "As quarterback, I really want to be an effective team leader. Do you have any words of wisdom for me?"

"Ah, leadership. That's one of my favorite subjects," Mo said. "I have a saying on my blog: Being a leader doesn't give you the freedom to do what you want, it gives you the power to do what you ought. Lead with integrity, lead with courage, lead with humility. In a nutshell, be a leader worth following...."

Coach led the applause, and everyone followed. "Thank you so much, Mo, for being here and for your great advice."

Thursday. His second Thursday in a row without a JV game. Chase could get used to this, and he was finally getting caught up in algebra. Tripp was coming to more and more classes, but he hardly spoke in class, and certainly never said anything to Chase. For as much fun as it was getting ready for the varsity playoffs, he was sad that he wasn't doing it alongside Tripp. Should he have told Todd, the trainer, about Tripp? Tripp's parents thought so, but life sure would be easier if he hadn't.

Practice was a simple affair. No tackling and not much hitting. It had been a long season, and Coach Skalaski wanted them fresh. They ran through a variety of plays, and then Coach spoke to the team.

"We've been through a lot this year. We've played some teams that weren't very good, and some teams that are great. All I ask of you tomorrow is that you do what you've done all year: play hard and smart. We'll be just fine."

The other guys seemed fine, but Chase was wired.

It was another night of restlessness. Chase had a tricky time falling asleep.

Friday started out well enough. Hannah hadn't had

any nightmares lately. Chase wondered if it was since their dad hadn't called again. Mr. Stevens had called his dad with tickets and sure enough, his dad hadn't called Chase back since.

He found himself praying more. For Hannah not to worry or have bad dreams. For his dad to call more. For Tripp to start talking to him.

For him to worry less. *It was slow going, getting your prayers answered*, he thought.

His mom was up early, up and about, worrying about him eating. He just wasn't that hungry, and Daisy was glad. She seemed glad that it was gameday, since a waffle and two pieces of sausage all came her way.

At school, he found himself with butterflies all day. He tried to focus in class and it worked, at least a little bit. He learned at least something, he thought. Hamburgers delivered by Duffy's, a local Lincoln hamburger joint, were the pregame meal. That seemed to cure his butterflies.

Surprisingly, on Friday afternoon JB was the one with the jitters. He was as quiet as Chase had ever seen him during pregame meal. Chase had followed JB across the room where JB, for the first time this year, sat away from the rest of the team. Some players were the type to stay quiet and look anxious on game day, but Carr didn't have many like that. And JB certainly wasn't one of those — most weeks.

Everyone else seemed relatively laid-back as usual.

Chris and Will Kingston were at another table laughing with Solomon Williams and the other linemen, but JB walked past them to sit elsewhere. Chase walked up behind JB, and realized that JB was even dressed differently than normal. He was wearing jeans, as he usually did, a deep, dark blue pair, but wore a white crisp button-down shirt, instead of his usual, casual long-sleeved shirts that he wore. Strangely enough, no vest today.

"Mind if I join you? If it's okay with you." He had wondered sometimes why JB had started to take such an interest in him, coming to his JV games, then seemingly always looking for him during team meetings or at practice to offer a helpful comment, or sometimes just a funny one probably to loosen him up. Maybe he could repay the favor by sitting with JB.

JB smiled. "Yes, of course." Chase sat down across from JB.

JB grinned, but it wasn't as quick and open of a smile as usual. He always had a smile, but today it seemed strained, like he was forcing himself to do it. "You were wearing a Lecrae shirt yesterday, I noticed."

Chase looked down and nodded. "Yeah, I heard about him recently. From somewhere." He grinned and JB laughed. Both boys knew that Chase had no idea who the Christian rap artist was until dinner at JB's house.

Chase grinned, then tried to make his face serious.

"No way, man. I'm clearly my own guy." Both boys laughed again but JB's smile quickly faded.

"Are you okay?" asked Chase.

"Yes," said JB. "I'm just a little nervous about tonight." Chase was surprised. Surprised that JB was nervous and that he was so open about it.

JB continued. "About the game, a little. But then also about the scouts and what all that means." Chase looked puzzled — he didn't understand why JB was suddenly worried. JB smiled, a little. "Coaches from Ohio State and Miami are coming over, and Georgia and Kentucky and a couple others, maybe — Michigan State, too, has coaches coming. And for the first time, at least the first time to see me in person, Florida will have a coach there too."

"Well, that's great! Those are terrific options," said Chase. "You nervous because they'll all be there to watch?"

"A little, I guess. No, no, not really. I feel good about Coach's game plan and really the name of the game is about us winning. It'll go well enough for me and for us and we'll win. And that's what's really important about tonight. Playing as well as we can, and winning."

"Well, sure, but you want to play well too," said Chase.

"Sure I do," said JB. "I want to play in a manner worthy of the gospel."

Chase felt like he should know what that meant, but really had no clue. And since JB was being so talkative, he figured he'd go ahead and ask — and it would keep JB talking, which seemed to be good for JB. "What's that mean, to play in a manner worthy of the gospel?"

"It means playing within the rules. It means not doing anything inappropriate or disrespectful. But more than that it means playing as hard as I can, for as long as I can. The point is, God gave me certain abilities. There are some things that I do better than other people."

Chase grinned. There were a *lot* of things JB did better than most people.

"God made me fast. God made me strong. And I've improved on some of those things by working. Have you ever seen *Chariots of Fire*?" Chase shook his head no. "Well, it's like that. There was an Olympic runner, Eric Liddle, who said that God made him to run, and so he ran because he loved it, but also because doing it gave him joy because he was using those gifts that God gave him. I feel that joy when I play football. So, as long as I do everything I can to glorify God, then I'm satisfied with my performance."

"So, wait. I guess I don't get why you're still nervous?"

"It's all starting to get real," said JB. "Next year feels really close, but I have no idea what I want to do. The Gators, for instance, have been talking to me to play basketball. But not really football. I think that's okay. I think I'd rather play basketball, at least there. Or, do I want to play *both* sports somewhere?"

"The problem is playing two sports — or even just playing one sport in college — takes a lot of time. And I've got to make sure that I learn while I'm in school. Like my dad did. So, do I want to play two sports, or take a shot at one, or I could even go to an Ivy League school and not worry about sports." Chase whistled softly.

"I've heard you were smart," Chase said. "But I'd never really seen any evidence of that, so I thought they were lying." Chase said facetiously as JB chuckled.

"Yeah, Harvard, Princeton, Penn, and a couple of others have been calling me as well." He looked around and lowered his voice. "But you don't need to tell anyone that. I don't know how the names of the other schools got out — I guess from the coaches telling reporters — but I don't want anyone to ever think I'm bragging about it. So, I'm hoping nobody hears about it. *I'm* not going to be the one to tell them." His voice returned to a normal level. "My folks really want me to go to an Ivy League school. And I really like that idea too."

"It kind of feels like a good problem to have. Plus, you'll get your school paid for," Chase added.

"Right. Sure. A good problem," said JB. "Actually, it's a *great* problem, and I kind of feel guilty that it's making me nervous. Yeah, it's definitely a good problem." JB looked around and realized they were the last ones in the room. "Let's get out of here. Let's go beat the Rams." He grinned and hopped up, then sat back down before Chase even stood up. "We've been talking about me the whole time. What about you? Things better with Tripp?"

"No, not at all." Actually, the last two days, Chase had started to feel a little better. He'd talked with his mom for a while on Wednesday night about Tripp and was spending more time with Hannah. There was only so much he could do. He'd done the right thing in the first place. He'd told the truth. Tried to keep Tripp safe too.

They got to the locker room and Chase quickly dressed in his uniform pants and slipped on the blue "Stay Together" T-shirt that Coach had given them, which he was going to keep on under his shoulder pads. He left the locker room, carrying his shoulder pads, helmet, and other items together for the bus ride to Citizens Field in Gainesville.

It was a short ride back down 301 to the scene of his JV game against Buchholz.

The stadium at Citizens Field was different than most; it was surrounded by a chain link fence. That wasn't completely unusual, but the stands were also fenced in half, so that fans couldn't pass back and forth between the sides of the stadium. Whichever side a fan came in on, they were stuck on that side of the stadium for the whole game. The West side was for the visiting team, while the East was for the home team.

Appropriately enough, Carr's parents had set up their blue and green banners on the West side, while the orange and green of Eastside was on the … East side.

But tonight, only one side mattered. JB's side.

Maybe JB was one of those people for whom a case of nerves helped him play better, because on this night, he was *amazing*. Coaches from Florida, FSU, Michigan State, Duke, Miami, Kentucky, Penn, Penn State, and Princeton marveled at his football exploits.

JB ran for one touchdown, and had thrown for six more.

In the first half.

49 – 0, Carr led at halftime.

Coach Quinn, the offensive coordinator, took JB aside at halftime. "We're going to take you out and keep you healthy and play Roger in the second half."

"Great. Absolutely, Coach." Coach Quinn went off to speak with Roger about the second half.

Chase heard his name called early in the third quarter from someone in the stands. Unlike JB, who always had people calling to him from the stands, half of them holding up signs of various colleges they hoped JB would play for, this was new for Chase, so he turned. It was Theo Chuang, a student who wrote for the school newspaper.

"Chase!" Theo called out, waving him over. Theo was at the bottom of the stands, but couldn't get any closer because of the fence around the field. Chase looked around and figured it was all right, then trotted over to the bottom of the stands. He looked up at Theo.

"JB has six passing touchdowns already, is he going back in the game at all?" Along with everyone else, Theo had seen Roger Dalton go into the game to start the second half.

"I don't know," said Chase, running a hand through his brown hair, pushing it back over his eyes. "I doubt it, though."

"They've got to put him back in! With one more touchdown pass he will tie Tim Tebow and others for second place in the Florida record books, and the state record is only eight by a guy from Orlando."

Chase shrugged. He didn't know what to do.

"Well, at least go tell somebody. Make sure they know."

Chase walked away slowly. He knew he didn't want to go talk with Coach Skalaski about it. He wasn't sure what Coach would think of talk of individual records, especially during a game. He had a guess that it wouldn't be good. But then again, Coach Skalaski loved JB. Chase decided to start by telling JB and walked over to the senior quarterback. JB was watching from the sideline with his shoulder pads and helmet off.

"Hey, Chase. Been talking to your fans?" JB flashed his grin.

Chase was about to grow flustered, then realized that he had the perfect response. For once. "No, I was talking with one of *your* fans. Theo Chuang said that with one more touchdown pass tonight you will tie Tim Tebow for second in the Florida record books, and with two more you will tie the all-time state record."

JB grinned. "Cool." He didn't move.

"So ... shouldn't you grab your pads and go back in?"

"No, I don't think I need to be tying Tim Tebow. Some records don't need to be broken." He grinned. "Plus, putting Roger into the game was the right thing to do, the sportsmanlike thing to do. So me being out is *still* the right thing to do, even now that we know this. Any records won't matter. The right thing is still the right thing. And, you know, Roger has worked really hard and been dedicated to this team. It's important that he get to play."

By the end of the third quarter, Eastside had scored three times to cut the lead to 49 – 21. Two of those touchdowns came after Roger threw two interceptions, and the third came after Roger fumbled. The poor guy was having a horrible game. Or at least, a horrible third quarter.

Coach Skalaski walked over to JB and told him to get his pads and helmet back on.

After a few minutes, Coach Skalaski yelled, "JB!"

JB ran over to Coach. "Coach, I'll do it. I'll do whatever you say. But even if they score, we're still up by three touchdowns. I think Roger can — actually, Roger *needs* — to finish this game. Maybe for Carr later this season, but mostly for Roger for the rest of his life. He can do this, and needs to realize that he can bounce back from this moment. But ... you decide."

Coach Skalaski was quiet, then nodded. "Just stay ready." Then he turned from JB and yelled again. "Roger! Let's work on some stuff! Let's talk about the next plays we're going to run when you go back in!"

On the next drive, Roger led the Loggerheads down the field, and Megan kicked a forty-four yard field goal to add to the lead. 52 – 28. Eastside would end up scoring one more time, but Roger finished the game, JB stayed on the sidelines, and Carr won, 52 – 35.

Chase played on the kickoff team again, and he didn't make any tackles. But no one ran any kicks back to the 10-yard line, either.

CHAPTER 18

It was Monday afternoon and spirits were high after the playoff win over Eastside. As usual, Chase tried to be one of the first players into the locker room. He would dress and sit in his locker chatting with the other guys.

Today, however, he was running late. His recent study habits had finally caught up with him. He'd done poorly on an English test—a 72—and Mrs. Brantley, his teacher, was concerned because he was one of her stronger students. She asked him to meet her after school for a few minutes to review the test and make corrections. When he finally raced into the locker room, he expected to find it empty and most guys already gone and onto the field. Instead, it was packed; the other players were gathered around in a group, excited voices rising. He worked his way into the circle, as guys had their backs to him.

"What's going on?" Chase asked.

"Roger Dalton went up to the minimart," Dimitri said. "He got a gallon of milk and he's betting us he can drink it in thirty minutes."

"Really? A gallon? I guess he could ..." Chase's voice trailed off as he looked from the gallon of milk on a table to Roger, the face of the senior grinning and carefree. Chase again looked at the gallon. Roger's face looked a little mean under that grin, but maybe it was Chase's imagination.

"Okay," he said. "What are people betting?"

Will leaned in and said quietly, "Nothing, really. Roger made it sound like a bet, but he just wants to do it. There are about five dimes on the table — they may all be Roger's." Chase looked over and saw the coins on the edge of the table.

Roger looked at Chase with a smirk. "It's about $37, I think." But Roger laughed as he said it and the others joined in. Roger was just being snarky. "I'm gonna go ahead in a minute. You want to add something? I've got to get started, but if the payoff isn't high enough, I may not do it at all."

Chase could tell that Roger would do it anyway. *He'd do it for free for the attention*, Chase thought. Chase shook his head no, then put his hands in his pockets as if he was checking for change. He found a stick of gum and decided to throw it on the table. *Take that, Roger.*

Five dimes and a piece of Trident.

Roger grinned then checked his watch. He was already in his uniform ready for practice. "Practice starts in twenty-eight minutes and it'll take a minute or two to get out to the field, so I've got to drink this in twenty-six minutes?"

Chase nodded. He saw Will across the crowd and started walking over as Roger tipped his head back and put the gallon of milk to his lips. "Well, here he goes," Chase said. Voices got louder.

Will grinned. "Yeah, I can't imagine having a gallon of milk in your stomach at all. What he really hasn't thought about is going out to practice with it in there. *That's* when he's going to feel terrible."

"That's a good point. It'll be worth it just to watch him." Chase responded. "I've never heard of something like this, though. I'll bet he's already done it before. It's probably not that hard."

Roger stopped drinking and wiped his mouth with the back of his hand. The milk had gone down about two inches. Roger paused.

"Twenty-five minutes," someone announced. Roger tipped the milk back again, putting it to his mouth. Chase and Will watched, cheered, and laughed with the other guys for the next fifteen minutes until just a scant amount remained at the bottom of the jug.

Chase looked around the room. Tripp wasn't there, of course. He hadn't been cleared by the doctors to practice so he didn't want to come at all, his dad had said. *Tripp would like this*, Chase thought. He felt sad.

Roger sat down on the table. "I don't know, guys. I don't know how I'm going to practice with all this in my stomach," he said.

Several guys called out. "Hurry up." "Keep going!" "Hurry!" they yelled.

Roger picked up the jug, but the carefree grin was gone. His face now looked pained. Drawn. And a little bit white. His usual surfer's tan had faded, replaced by a clammy shade of pale. Roger tipped it to his mouth, finishing the milk in several swallows.

Just then, Coach Skalaski walked into the room. "Guys, we've got practice in four minutes and I don't have ONE GUY OR GAL ON THE FIELD! What is going ... oh, my. Roger, what are you —"

Roger leaned forward and milk began flying out of his mouth like a shot out of a fireman's hose toward a burning building. Coach jumped back, his shoes covered.

"What in the wor —"

Guys were laughing hysterically. Roger was bent over as milk kept coming and coming. Chase said to Will, "My word. That has to be the *whole* gallon."

"It is!" yelled Will to his brother, who was standing beside them. "It is! Chris, that's the *whole* gallon." Chris

195

looked at the giant puddle spreading out across the tile floor and spoke calmly.

"Yes, I believe that it is."

Chase hadn't been seeing much progress in the relationship between him and Tripp, but he was somewhat encouraged the next morning, Tuesday.

Tripp had begun riding his bike to school again, but wouldn't ride with Chase. Chase had waited for him a couple of mornings, watching Tripp on his bike, in his garage, waiting for Tripp to ride up. It was only when Chase had given up and begun pedaling that Tripp began riding as well, keeping well behind Chase on the bike path. Chase stopped, giving Tripp a chance to catch up, but each time Tripp had stopped too, until Chase started riding again. After being tardy twice in a row, Chase decided to just go on without Tripp.

Then Tripp had come over that day and sat behind Chase in algebra. It wasn't *next* to Chase as before, but Chase took it as a good sign maybe the ice was thawing between them. Maybe they'd be able to speak soon. They weren't able to talk that day in class, because Mr. Payne was giving a test. By the time class was over, Tripp was gone.

The mood was upbeat at practice on Tuesday afternoon. Maybe too upbeat. They caught a break when Raines was upset in the first round by Cocoa Beach, so Carr wouldn't have to face Raines again just a few weeks after Raines had beaten them so badly. Instead, they were traveling to play at Cocoa Beach that Friday.

Sure enough, the players were having trouble focusing on Cocoa Beach, and about ten minutes into practice, while still in individual drills, Coach Skalaski's whistle brought everything to a screeching halt. He called them to midfield, and they gathered around him.

"You won last week! You guys do understand that it was *last* week? You can't roll over points in the playoffs from week to week?" He looked around, his eyes dark and intense. "That is, we can't 'roll over' our extra points from last week! We have to start at *zero* against Cocoa Beach. We don't get to use any of the points we got last week. Those are over. And guess what? These guys are good enough that they *beat* Raines, which we couldn't do!"

Chase could tell that Coach was frustrated. "In fact, you guys got so pleased with yourselves in the second half that we almost let Eastside come back! As I told you then, a win is a win. There are no style points. Just win the game.

"But, as I have said time and again, we need to do things the *right way*. Each time, *every* time. Then, the winning will take care of itself. We did that for the first half, but not the second.

"Now get back to work!" Coach blew his whistle, restarting practice. The rest of practice was as intense as any they'd had since Chase was called up to varsity.

After the rough beginning to practice the day before, which had ended with hard sprints, Chase groaned at Wednesday's alarm, threw his legs over the side of the bed, and promptly stepped on Hannah.

Hannah grunted then yelped. Chase quickly became fully awake.

"Sorry, Sis." He now realized that she was there, using the blanket he had been keeping down at the front of his bed, and had brought her pillow with her. "You had that dream again?"

Hannah nodded. "I'm sick of it," she said. He nodded. Hannah had always sensed that Chase was her ally in life. He was the one person who she would always be able to hang onto—she knew that from when she was little. That's part of why they hardly fought even though they were different ages, but in the same grade.

Hannah knew that her parents were there for her too, but even before their dad had walked out she had felt the bond that exists between siblings to be very strong between her and her brother. She adored her mother, and during the time in Lincoln the three of them had grown even closer and couldn't be separated.

But, then, the dreams started one night.

"The graveyard again?" Chase asked.

Hannah nodded.

"But you can't tell where, or what's going on?"

Hannah shook her head.

"You don't know, or you don't want to talk about it?"

"Both," she answered. She pulled the blanket tighter. Chase sat there on the side of the bed, the younger brother, not sure what to do. The graveyard was somewhere she'd never seen before. As best she could tell, it had a handful of tombstones but mostly had markers laid out flat in the grass and a smooth mound of dirt. In each dream, Hannah smoothed the dirt with her shoe, using her instep, dragging and smoothing. And each time Chase would walk up, put his arm around her, and not say a word.

"Did I say anything?" Chase asked.

"No," she answered, her voice barely a whisper.

Nobody ever spoke in the dream.

They had gone to church more or less over the years, probably more in recent years than when they were in Atlanta, and Hannah believed in Heaven. The dream was upsetting and caused her to wake up and wonder. She knew each time it was *only* a dream, but she still needed to come into Chase's room for comfort. Never their mom's room, always his.

The one good thing was that it made her feel closer to Chase each time. And so she would get out of her bed and walk into his room. She knew that she and

Chase were going to go through life together, and weather the ups and downs as siblings.

"I wish you didn't have that dream, Hannah," Chase said.

Hannah nodded, then shrugged. "It's not that big of a deal. It's just a dream. This is really just a reminder that you're here and you're my brother." Chase smiled.

After that beginning, the rest of the day seemed fine. He still wasn't exactly sure what was going on in algebra, but he'd catch up soon enough. There and in English too.

Friday. Gameday. No word from Tripp and on Wednesday Chase finally gave up. He'd walked over one day the week before but he only spoke with Tripp's parents. They were as baffled as he was with Tripp's behavior. But what could *he* do? He'd tried a couple more times this week and then decided to leave it alone and surrender it to God. Clearly, Tripp needed space. *So much for sitting behind me in algebra. Maybe it wasn't a positive sign.*

The team left school early, late in the morning, for the drive down to Cocoa Beach.

After a couple of hours came the announcement from the front of the bus.

"We have driven slightly past Cocoa Beach High School."

He heard some laughter and some groans from the

bus and Coach Skalaski — the speaker in front — raised his hands.

"Hold on now, fellows," he said. "I'm kidding — kind of. This was on purpose." The prior season, Will had told Chase that they were headed to a game in Interlachen, and the bus driver got lost. After the bus driver claimed he was taking a shortcut for thirty minutes, Coach Skalaski who had made the trip numerous times, ended up directing the beleaguered driver to the stadium.

Coach Skalaski continued speaking to the team. "We have driven to Sebastian Inlet. Sebastian Inlet happens to be home of *the* Archie Carr National Wildlife Refuge, the largest protected area for turtles in the United States.

"Turtles, like loggerheads."

Guys cheered.

"Archie Carr, like Carr High School."

More cheers.

"Look, we don't have long, but spend a few minutes. We were too close not to stop," Coach said.

A park ranger stepped onto the bus and spoke to them for a moment to tell them a bit about where they were.

"There's a twenty-mile long beach here, designed for turtles to have a safe place to land, and we're going to let you look around."

They spent half an hour walking around the visitor's

area, and looking at the beach and the blue-gray waters of the Atlantic Ocean beyond.

"Where are the turtles?" asked Roger.

The park ranger smiled. "There aren't any to see here, at least not during the day. The refuge is supposed to give turtles a nice quiet, dark place they can come up on shore and lay their eggs — that's the only time they come on land."

They looked at exhibits about green sea turtles, and most of the players spent the bulk of their time looking at the information on loggerheads.

"Five minutes, guys!" Coach Skalaski called. "We're leaving in five minutes. Get on the bus or get left for the turtles!" Guys began filing back onto the buses — offensive guys on bus one, the defensive guys on bus two.

Before he climbed back on the bus, Chase walked away from the other players in the parking lot, behind bus one. He pulled out his cell phone. He didn't use it much. Even so, occasionally his mom would check his texts and other history, not as much to check on him, but it was his mother's way of checking to make sure that nobody was trying to reach out to him in a bad way. He didn't mind.

He called Hannah. "How's everything?" She filled him in on her day. "Sounds boring. Hey, heard anything about Tripp?" He couldn't help himself. It felt lousy, being in Cocoa Beach for a playoff game without Tripp.

"No. Sorry. Hey, wanna see a movie this weekend?"

He knew she was being nice, keeping him busy to keep his mind off of Tripp.

"Maybe so. Yeah, sounds good. Look, I'd better go. We're down in Cocoa Beach — we'll be home late."

"Good luck!"

The players hopped back on the buses and drove twenty minutes back *north* to Cocoa Beach.

As it turned out, they wouldn't need good luck, or any luck at all. The Minutemen of Cocoa Beach never knew what hit them. Cocoa Beach had a full stadium, and a raucous crowd dressed up in school colors of red, white, and blue. Coach Skalaski's worries about his players' focus after the Eastside win were decidedly put to rest. The week before, Cocoa had ground out a tough, upset victory over top-ranked Raines, surprising the Vikings and everyone else in the state, 20 – 17. However, they were not about to duplicate that feat. Not on this night.

Dimitri Anderson ran the opening kickoff back for a touchdown, Megan Brown added the extra point, and Carr led Cocoa Beach 7 – 0 after 13 seconds.

It was downhill from there for the Minutemen. Nick Wood intercepted a pass from the Cocoa Beach quarterback, and returned it twenty-six yards for a Carr touchdown. Megan trotted out and made it 14 – 0. In high school, teams were lucky to have kickers make half of the extra points. Megan made all of them, all year!

And then, minutes later, Carr got the ball on offense

for the first time. JB took the shotgun snap, and executed *Solo Left 13 Read* perfectly.

It was the mirror image of *Solo Right 12 Read*, which JB had been running effectively all year, including against Union County on the final drive. The coaches simply mixed in *Left 13* to the other side to keep defenses "honest," and from guessing.

JB read the right defensive end who did crash down hard, and kept the ball running for a 62-yard TD. And Megan added the extra point.

Of course.

21 – 0. Cocoa Beach began moving the ball with some success, and while they couldn't score, they at least chewed up some time on the clock and escaped at halftime trailing by that same three-touchdown deficit.

Most of the third quarter zipped by. Megan added two more field goals. JB threw a touchdown pass to Jackson, the junior who had replaced Tripp in the starting lineup, and was playing fairly well in his absence.

Seeing Jackson make the catch, and knowing that it could have been Tripp, saddened Chase despite his surroundings, standing in full uniform on the bright lights of a field, in a state playoff game. The reality was that he hadn't spoken to Tripp in three weeks. He missed Tripp, his mom and dad, and Kayla. Missed hanging out with him. He saw the other Stevens when he'd stop by, or see Tripp in class, but Tripp ignored Chase, which hurt a lot. Tripp seemed fully healed for class, but the doctors wouldn't let him participate in football yet, so he was still bitter.

Early in the fourth quarter, disaster struck. JB's foot got caught in a pile of players, and Todd ran out to check on JB as he was rolling around in pain. Roger went in and played quarterback for most of the fourth quarter, which was uneventful.

Chase kept looking back to the bench, watching Todd work on JB's ankle. JB seemed to be in a fair amount of pain.

Finally, with time running down, in between plays on offense, Coach sent Chase and the younger players into the game. Roger and other seniors could run off the field and out of the game in front of the handful of Carr fans who were there and stayed at the game long after many of the Cocoa Beach fans had headed for the exits.

Chase was excited to go in for the last three plays. Even though they were lining up in 'victory formation' where he takes the snap and kneels on the ball to run time off the clock, he was glad to get in the game.

In the end, the final score was 34 – 0 in favor of Archie F. Carr High School. Throw in the visit to the Archie Carr National Wildlife Refuge as well, and it was a very special day, indeed.

They headed back to Lincoln, exhausted and far too quiet for a team that had just won another playoff game. The team was thinking about JB's ankle. Was it broken? Chase's mind flipped from JB to Tripp and the excitement he felt earlier seemed long ago. He tried to get it back, thinking about the game, but he was tired. It didn't work. He tried to think about going to see a movie with Hannah on Saturday, but that wasn't making him feel much better, either.

CHAPTER 19

Hannah, Kate, Megan, Chase, and his mom rode in silence most of the way to Gainesville. It was movie matinee day, but Chase was kind of bummed since Tripp was still refusing to see him. Plus, he was nervous with Kate there, even with Megan and Hannah in the car.

Chase's mom broke the icy silence with a typical parent-y question: "So, what's going on in school? Anything good lately?"

"Not really," said Hannah. "We had an algebra test last week."

"How'd it go?"

"Pretty well," Hannah said.

"Chase? How'd you do?"

Chase jumped. "Do *what*? Sorry, I mean, excuse me?"

"Your algebra test," his mom explained. "How'd it go last week?"

"Fine," Chase said, then after a moment, added, "I'm pretty sure I missed a couple, but I think I did okay." He was glad she hadn't pressed the issue. He'd catch up.

They pulled up in front of an ice cream store that shared a parking lot with the movie theater. Mrs. Clark called out through the driver-side window as the kids got out, "I'll be back before the movie is over. I'll be parked right over there."

Chase held the door to the ice cream shop for the girls before entering and practically bumped right into Ken Block, his mom's musician friend.

"Hi, Mr. Block," said Chase, a little off guard.

Ken's face broke into a big grin. "Hey, Chase, good to see you! And, look, you don't have to call me 'Mr. Block.' Just call me 'Ken,' if that's Okay with you." Chase knew his mom would definitely want him to respectfully call him "*Mr.* Ken."

Chase introduced his sister, "This is Hannah."

Hannah seemed weird, star-struck. She spoke, her voice rising a little, as she grabbed hold of Kate's elbow. "My friend here and I are huge Sister Hazel fans! I recognize you from your *Release* CD cover. We love that one."

"Fantastic! We've been trying to make a fan out of Chase, but I'm not sure how that's going yet," Ken teased. Chase blushed.

"You *know* him?" Hannah asked Chase.

"Mom does," Chase whispered, trying to play it cool. "And *you're* a fan — who knew?"

Hannah turned directly toward Ken. "Kate turned me on to your music, just recently. Right, Kate?" Kate nodded, speechless.

"Well, it's so cool to run into some real fans. Oh, looks like I'm up." Ken ordered a double scoop of cookies-n-cream in a waffle cone, and waved goodbye as he left. "Great to meet you, kids!"

Hannah jumped up and down. "Chase, Mom knows him? *How?*"

"I don't know, she went to school with him or something."

Chase and the girls ordered, then took a table. Kate marveled, "I can't believe we just met Sister Hazel's lead singer! That is *so cool*. And your mom is friends with him? Even cooler!"

Meantime, Chase couldn't shake the worries about his best bud. Despite deciding to give the whole thing with Tripp to God, he'd made one last effort to speak with him Sunday. He worried that every day they didn't speak, it would get harder for things to ever get back to normal.

Tripp opened the door just as Chase was about to

knock. *Maybe that's a good sign*, Chase thought. *Or coincidence?*

"Why are *you* here?" Tripp asked. "Shouldn't you be with your new best friend, wrapping his ankle or something?"

Tripp closed the door, leaving Chase standing alone on the porch. "God?" Chase said out loud. "He's all yours!"

The rest of Sunday was a blur. Tripp was still angry.

Tripp was in algebra class Monday morning, sitting next to Kate again, no longer sitting behind Chase. He wasn't talking to her, though, Chase noticed. In fact, he wasn't talking to anyone.

Things were definitely different. Tripp was usually the life of the party, friendly with everyone. Now he seemed withdrawn and didn't talk much. Their other classes were the same. He never sat next to Chase in any class. And he didn't speak. He didn't whisper to Chase or anyone else, he didn't raise his hand like he used to in Coach Preston's American history class.

Tripp just walked in, sat down, and stayed quiet.

Weird.

After watching film Monday afternoon, the team stretched in silence, and went through their initial warm-ups. Chase began taking snaps from one of the centers alongside Roger. There were only two centers, but now there were only two quarterbacks too, with JB hurt. Before they started the team part of a short practice, Coach Skalaski gathered the team.

"Guys, there are times in life when you have to press ahead. Sometimes people let you down, sometimes things don't go right."

He stopped and looked at the faces surrounding him. Long faces. Sad faces. He switched his tone up a bit, trying to become more encouraging.

"But life goes on. Now, we're going to get ready to play Pahokee High. Roger is our guy. Roger has worked hard and learned a lot and will do a great job for us. He's been here four years. He knows this. Roger, your job is to focus this week on what we need to do and do the little things well. Not to do anything extraordinary, not to be James Brown, but to be the best *Roger* you can be on Friday night." Roger nodded. Around the circle, faces were still long and sad.

"Guys, that's the last I'm going to say about this. We're going to battle with the guys you see here. We've been getting ready for this game for a year and this time, we'll prevail."

JB grinned and nodded. "Roger, you can do it." Chase nodded and Roger grinned at him.

"Thanks, Squirt," Roger said.

Suddenly "Squirt" didn't seem so bad.

CHAPTER 20

The small town of Pahokee is a long way from Lincoln. It is located almost five hours away, through a series of state roads. Not a straight drive to get there. Not only is it a long distance away, it's a long time away. As in, it's from another time, a town from another era.

The year before, in the second round of the playoffs, Carr faced off against the Pahokee Blue Devils down in Pahokee. JB told Chase about their bus ride down there—Coach Skalaski took them to see the town of Pahokee and then Lake Okeechobee on the way to the game, on one of his field-trippy "wrong" turns.

Pahokee is a tiny town on the edge of Lake Okeechobee, the large lake that stands out like a large blue marble on maps of Florida. It is the seventh largest lake in the United States and the second largest totally within the United States, after only Lake Michigan. It's a shallow, marshy lake only thirteen feet down at its deepest point. Full of alligators and other wildlife. It may only be a few miles between the towns of Pahokee and glitzy Palm Beach on the Atlantic Ocean, just north of Miami, but it is light years removed.

Pahokee is an agricultural town, with many of its residents employed by "Big Sugar," the sugar industry of South Florida which grows sugar cane on the edge of the Everglades. Many of its businesses have slowed or have gone completely out of business, and the town has seen some tough days.

Remarkably, Pahokee, along with Belle Glade next door, turns out a surprising number of professional players for a town its size. The entire community of Pahokee has been able to rally around the Blue Devils football team, which has won six state championships in the last twenty years, including five in recent years. A very impressive run.

Carr had run into the Pahokee buzzsaw the year before, and Coach Skalaski was hopeful that they could reverse the result this year. Losing JB put a huge dent in that. He was a great talent, but just as important, his injury could be a huge distraction. Hopefully, the fact that Pahokee had to make the five-hour bus ride to come play in Lincoln this year would even things a bit.

Chris and Will Kingston, the twins, came to the rescue for the team at practice Tuesday. They were natural, quiet leaders, always doing the right thing. That week, they decided to talk more and urge on the others.

They were big enough to be noticed. As offensive linemen they needed to have large bodies, playing guard and tackle on the left side of the line. Will was slightly larger and played tackle, while Chris played just inside of him at guard. The boys stood out a little in Lincoln. Their dad was second-generation Chinese-American, and their faces showed it. When they were younger, this caused an occasional ruckus or two in school. Early on, they decided not to be fighters and had simply made fun of bullies with their quick comebacks. Everyone liked the Kingstons.

This week they were constantly urging players to run faster and practice harder.

"Look, guys, we've got to practice every play this week harder and faster than we ever do. The better we know our plays, the harder we practice, and the faster and better we will play on Friday," Chris said at one point as the offense was waiting for the team period to start.

Will chimed in. "And you've got to study your playbooks."

Each week, the coaches gave the players a small three-ring binder that consisted of a handful of plays pulled from the large playbook. Coach Skalaski never wanted them to worry about *all* the plays in the large playbook. He thought they could run several plays more effectively if they practiced only those few that week, and knew them well. Therefore, each week, he cut down the large playbook to those that the coaches thought would work best against the next opponent. Occasionally, he might use one or two other plays, but not often.

JB once told Chase that Coach Skalaski and Coach Preston had debated this point during a timeout once last year. Coach Preston said *Rex Gun 200 Flood* would be the perfect play against the defense they were facing late in the game. Coach Skalaski agreed but said that he wouldn't run it. They hadn't practiced it. Coach Skalaski said he'd rather use a play they practiced and that the players would know without thinking. JB said Coach Skalaski's decision had worked out for the best, and Carr had gone on to win the game.

Will continued talking to the team. "You've got to know your plays this week. You've got to know them inside and out. Roger will, Chris will, and I will. The rest of you have to know them as well as you know your phone number."

Practice picked up from that point. Coach Skalaski stood back and watched the Kingstons talk to their teammates. It was the first time he'd had hope that they might be able to beat Pahokee.

JB took him aside a little later during a water break. Chase wasn't sure what prompted it, but JB seemed to be pretty good at studying people.

"Chase," JB had said, "if you are important, then you're important. You're not important because you're playing varsity, or because Kate notices you, or because Coach Skalaski says something nice in practice, or Coach Preston. If you have value, then you *have value*. And, *you* have value. So don't go looking to everyone else to try to find that value. Sometimes, it'll be there. Sometimes, sadly, it won't, but what makes you important isn't out there." JB had pointed out in different directions as he said the words "out there." "It's in *here*," and he pointed at his heart. "People look at the outward appearance, but God looks at the heart."

Chase spent the week running the Scout Team offense, but also got a few snaps with the actual offense. He was, after all, now the backup quarterback with Roger starting and JB out.

Those few snaps merely consisted of handing off. Running plays to the right, running plays to the left. Chase knew his role as the emergency quarterback. Hold things together until Roger could get back into the game. But at the same time, he was important. Chase was trying to remember that, that he was important on the inside whether he played much — or at all.

Friday morning rolled around. It was gameday against Pahokee. Chase had eaten breakfast. Hannah didn't have any nightmares. Even Daisy seemed satisfied with only two pieces of bacon. Chase was ready for the day!

Mrs. Brantley paused as the door to the hallway opened with fifteen minutes left in class. They were discussing Gandalf in *The Hobbit*, and the imagery Tolkien created in his Middle Earth fantasy. Finally wrapping up their reading of the book.

A student with an "Office Aide" name badge stepped inside the door.

"Mr. Sebring needs to see Chase Clark," the Office Aide said. Chase could feel all eyes turn toward him. He would have been embarrassed, but he had a new-found confidence now that he was playing varsity. It was the playoffs, and Chase could barely concentrate as it was. The thrill of being so close to the state championship game, and the excitement and terror of possibly playing quarterback, coupled with the anxiety from not having JB available to play was zapping his mental energy.

Chase was definitely feeling good, but distracted. It was such a good day that even having an Office Aide come for him seemed like another good thing. Anything to not have to sit still any longer! Chase started to stand and Mrs. Brantley nodded that he could go. He quickly grabbed *The Hobbit*, and tossed it into his open backpack.

"Carefully! Carefully! We treat books with care," Mrs. Brantley reminded him.

"Yes, ma'am." Chase placed *The Hobbit* with more care down into the backpack, slung the strap over his left shoulder, and headed out behind the Office Aide.

He certainly didn't expect to see his mom or Mr. and Mrs. Stephens already seated in the room. He turned and saw Tripp sitting in the corner. And Mr. Payne, their algebra teacher.

"I wish I could say it is a pleasure to see you, Mr. Clark." *Mr. Sebring certainly didn't mind starting a meeting on a bad tone*, Chase thought. He sat in the only open seat, next to Tripp.

"I am troubled by the most recent test in Algebra I Honors. To be exact, I am extremely troubled by the tests turned in by the two gentlemen here, Mr. Stevens and Mr. Clark." He looked at the two boys. "Tripp and Chase, that is."

Duh, thought Chase. But then he found himself terrified. *What was Mr. Sebring talking about?*

"Mr. Payne brought these tests to me late yesterday afternoon. I am trying not to jump to any conclusions, but at the moment I'm having a hard time finding a reasonable explanation that does *not* include cheating." Chase's stomach flipped.

Cheating! No way!

There was some mistake, or Mr. Payne got tests mixed up or something. There just was *no way*. Instead of defending himself, he sat there silently, feeling sick and frightened. But Tripp didn't stay quiet.

"This is ridiculous!" he shouted and stood up. "In fact, I'm not going to listen to you talk about us like – "

His dad's sharp voice cut Tripp off in midsentence. "Sit! We will hear from you in a moment. Do you understand?" Mr. Sebring nodded.

Tripp sat, but he still looked angry. Chase wished he felt angry, but right now he could feel nothing but a cold pit of dread in his stomach. He was frightened. There had to be some mistake. He had no idea what it was, or how to fix it.

Mr. Sebring grabbed several papers off his desk. Chase could see his own handwriting on the top one. "Mr. Payne, would you help me with these tests and show us what caught your attention?"

Mr. Payne's head nodded. He had short, dark hair, pale skin from spending too much time indoors, despite living in Florida. His dark beard contrasted with his pale skin.

Usually his beard looked cool. The boys loved him — he'd been a guide for river rafting on the Chatooga and other wild rivers, and the boys thought he was totally cool. A math teacher who had adventures!

Today, his features looked unusually harsh. The angles of his cheeks and nose came together more sharply than Chase remembered. His beard seemed dark and scary. Chase decided his mind was playing tricks on him. Maybe. Mr. Payne's eyes flashed as he took the test from Mr. Sebring. Chase could see that

Mr. Payne was angry too, and the pit grew colder and sank deeper into his stomach.

"Yes, Mr. Sebring. Here's what I saw. Number two was the first one that grabbed my attention." He went to the white board on the wall behind Mrs. Clark, and Chase turned to watch him write:

$$\#2) \ 5x + 8y = -57$$
$$-5x - 5y = 30$$

"We are working on solving simultaneous equations with X and Y variables and as you can see, this is pretty straightforward."

Chase wasn't sure why he was explaining all this. Maybe for his mom's benefit, or for the Stevens' benefit. He understood this stuff. It was the new stuff that he was falling behind on.

Mr. Payne continued. "All you have to do is add the two equations together such that – 5x plus 5x becomes zero x, and so the X term is no longer part of this problem." Chase was listening but not totally hearing any longer. He was still terrified. Meanwhile, Mr. Payne was still solving the problem. " ... then by adding 8y and minus 5y leaves 3y, and negative 57 is added to 30, leaving negative 27. So at this step, we should have 3y equals negative 27. Easy, right?"

Heads nodded but Chase wasn't sure if everyone was following. Obviously the answer was negative 9.

He was only nodding because he didn't want anyone to get angrier with him.

"That's not what Mr. Clark and Mr. Stevens had. Instead both took the same detour along the way, and instead of adding -57 and 30 to get -27 they apparently subtracted 30 from -57 and $3y$ equals -87. By then they were well off course and their answers reflected that. They had the wrong answer for Y and then the wrong answer when they plugged that into either initial equation to solve for X."

Ugh. Chase couldn't believe he'd done that. He knew, sitting here, that he should have added. Duh.

Chase finally found his voice and started to speak. It came out in a squeak.

"I know I wasn't studying as much as I should have been." He explained that with JV ending and his promotion to varsity he'd fallen behind. "Plus, I was catching up on an oral report for English. But, I know these should've been added together. I'm not sure what happened here."

He tried to continue, when Mr. Sebring looked right at him and said, "Do not interrupt Mr. Payne. We'll let you know when we want to hear from you." When he heard Mr. Sebring's tone, Chase focused on just not getting sick right there in the office.

Mr. Payne continued speaking. "One other student besides Tripp and Chase made the same mistake, so it's not unthinkable that this could happen. However, it happened again on number four, in which they had to determine whether an ordered pair was a correct solution for a pair of simultaneous equations." He wrote the problem on Mr. Sebring's whiteboard:

$$\#4)\ x + 3y = 10$$
$$4x - y = 14$$

a) $(4, 2)$

b) $(1, 3)$

c) $(-5, 5)$

"Here, you will see in number four, they were given two equations, then they were to figure out which of the three sets of ordered pairs were a correct answer, if any. Both boys got them wrong, in the same way. Not just the same answers, but when I examined the tests, I saw that the computations that they had jotted down alongside the problem were the same. Number five is another example, in which the same thing happened. Those are three specific examples, and it happened four *additional* times on the test. I could go through those remaining four, but I don't think I need to. I think the point is clear. They both got a sixty-four on the test, by identical means. They may as well have turned in one test with both names written on it, as far as I'm concerned."

The hits just kept coming, Chase thought. A 64% on a test. *They think I cheated my way to a 64%.* Good heavens. He would have been lucky if his only problem was not to be grounded from doing anything after school for weeks to come. But he was in unchartered waters with these claims of cheating on the test.

His mom might never let him leave his room again.

Except that it wasn't true. He just didn't know how to prove it. It certainly looked like they must have cheated after all that Mr. Payne had said. Chase didn't understand how he and Tripp, who hadn't spoken to him since the night they played the Bartram Trails Bears a month before, could have worked together on a test.

Mr. Sebring now spoke.

"Thank you, Alex." He smiled grimly at Mr. Payne, who nodded. "I think that is enough for me to hear for now." Mr. Sebring looked around the room, and Chase saw his mom and the Stevens all nod in agreement. Their faces were also grim and their mouths drawn tight. Mr. Sebring turned his short, red hair toward Chase.

"*Now*, Mr. Clark, you may respond if there is anything you would like to say."

And, of course, any and all words had left Chase by then. He began to stammer, saying that there had to have been some mistake. "I would never cheat," he said, and turned toward the Stevens. "You know that as well as my mom does. And ..." Words failed him and he felt his eyes welling up. "And you guys know — Tripp won't even speak to me. How could we have cheated?" Chase was trying not to cry. He just couldn't believe it. *What was happening?*

Chase turned to Mr. Sebring. "Ever since he got hurt, Tripp won't talk to me. That was back in October! How could we have worked together when we aren't even speaking?" Neither Mr. nor Mrs. Stevens would look directly at him. Mrs. Stevens glanced at him for a moment then quickly glanced away. Chase could tell that his mom, the tough single mother who was used to arguing cases in front of juries and negotiating deals with difficult attorneys, was on the verge of tears. He felt awful, but didn't know what to do or say. He couldn't figure out what had happened.

The room was still and silent. Finally, Mr. Sebring cleared his throat. "Tripp, do you have anything to say in your defense?" Tripp looked sullen and downcast, and Mr. Sebring spoke again. "Chase, I'm sorry to hear you denied this and continued on this path. It's pretty clear what happened. Let me suggest before you speak, Tripp, that if you have anything to say, if either one of you would like to say something besides just denying it, maybe we won't come down so hard on you."

Tripp suddenly spoke. "No, sir, I have no defense for our actions. We just made a mistake. We shouldn't have cheated, I guess the pressure got to us. We shouldn't have cheated," he said again.

Chase felt like he was going to faint. The room was

spinning. Mr. Sebring nodded, then like a judge, gave his verdict. At least, that's how it felt to Chase. It felt like he was watching one of his mom's trials, and now, he was about to be sentenced. Whatever he said or did wasn't going to make any difference. If anything, it sounded like every time he spoke, things got worse.

"Chase and Tripp, I am suspending you boys from school for cheating. You will both receive zeros on that test, instead of the sixty-four that Mr. Payne gave you. Chase, you will be out for the next ten days, and that suspension will include not only school but any sports or anything else."

Football. Tonight's game.

"Tripp, you will be suspended for seven days, because of your willingness to take responsibility. But you'll still have seven days out of school, because actions have consequences. We'll use this as a learning opportunity, but the fact remains that there are consequences even when you own up to your mistakes." Tripp nodded. Mr. Sebring turned to the parents.

"Do you all have any questions or anything further to discuss about this?"

All three adults shook their heads, but then Mr. Stevens spoke up. His words were awful to Chase's ears. Tripp didn't move a muscle as his dad spoke.

"Boys, I'm not sure I could be any more disappointed. Tripp, as your father, and Chase, since I feel like I *am* your father, and wish I *was* your father, I am shocked, horrified, sickened. All of that. And incredibly angry. We have told you that in all circumstances you are to be truthful. *The truth will set you free*. Tripp, I'm a little pleased that you have started down that path this morning by telling the truth today, but I'm still so unbelievably upset that you were willing to cheat. The main reason to go to school is to prepare you with lessons in knowledge of intellect, and character of the heart and mind. And in one fell swoop, in one moment of weakness, you boys *completely* failed on both accounts!"

His voice had been rising, and he paused to calm himself. "That is unacceptable. I know I speak for your mothers in saying that we still love you boys, but this *will not*, this *cannot* happen again. Do I make myself clear?"

Tripp and Chase nodded.

Mr. Sebring nodded toward Mr. Stevens.

"Thank you, Mr. Stevens. I truly couldn't have said that any better. Boys, I trust this will not happen again. Any further incidents will result in your expulsion from Carr High School, but I have no doubt that will never be an issue. Tripp, we will see you in seven days. Chase, we will see you the following week. There is paperwork for both families on your way out."

The nightmare in Mr. Sebring's office had finally come to a close, but Chase was sure there was more to follow. He could feel that cold dread deep in his bones, and somehow, he knew it wasn't over.

CHAPTER 21

Friday afternoon passed slowly, with every five minutes feeling like it had been an hour. Chase didn't help the time pass by any, just sitting in his room, staring at the walls. He was trying to read, but spent more time thinking about what he was missing that day than *The Hobbit*. He thought about the pregame meal, wondering whether it was barbecue or hamburgers or chicken. Morgen's BBQ or Duffy's.

He thought about dressing in the locker room, putting on the blue home jersey. He'd have loved to smell the locker room's awful stench of sweat and humidity. After the win over Cocoa Beach, he went online and bought special bright green wristbands and a green thin towel to hang from his belt. He looked over at his desk, where the towel and wristbands were hanging. They seemed sad and lonely to Chase. Or maybe he was. He continued moping, straining to think about what had gone wrong until he couldn't focus anymore.

He knew that replaying the events of the last few days wouldn't get him anywhere but he tried to figure it all out anyway. First, there had been JB's injury.

And then, this morning was truly unbelievable. Hadn't he and Tripp simply made the same mistakes on the test? They'd been friends for so long that they probably thought alike. Of course he hadn't cheated. He would never cheat.

As he left school he'd asked Tripp why he'd lied, and Tripp called *him* a liar. So much for things getting better.

Mr. Payne must have jumped to a conclusion based on a few similar answers, right? He needed to ask his mom to get both tests, and help them put together a defense. She did that for people all the time. She could be his lawyer too. He'd ask when she got home — yes, he'd ask her to be his lawyer. Chase finally had a little hope. Something was missing about the cheating. He could feel it even if he couldn't figure it out — yet. But his mom could.

A little while longer, although it felt like a long while longer for Chase, Hannah burst through the door, and his mother came in a few minutes later.

"There are frozen pizzas and frozen dinners in the outside freezer, Chase," his mother called as she headed past his room toward hers. "And don't stay up too late."

"Wait, what? Where you going? And what about Hannah? Is there enough dinner for both of us?" He knew there was plenty of food in the house for both he and Hannah, but he was fishing for information. He could tell they were both rushing around, but couldn't figure out where they were going. And he wanted to talk to her about forming a defense for him against the cheating charges.

"We're headed to the game," his mom called.

Chase groaned. *You have got to be kidding me*, he thought.

Instead, he said, "Seriously?"

"Yes," replied his mother. "We're grabbing jackets and heading out." The weather had finally changed for good in Lincoln, a week before Thanksgiving. The game would be chilly. Ten minutes later, they rushed past and Chase heard the car head down the driveway toward Carr and the Loggerheads' playoff game. This was so unfair.

Chase was left with nothing to do but sulk and stare at his towel and wristbands. He'd have to talk to his mom about a defense later. But it didn't sound like an easy talk.

Kickoff was at 7:30, forty-five minutes earlier. Chase was still on his bed. He'd moved from sulking to pouting. It was *so* unfair. His sister and mom had been gone for an hour. Even Daisy looked like she was pouting at how unfair Chase's life was.

Chase went out to his tree house to sit. And brood.

He read the permanent-marker graffiti he and Tripp had written on the inside walls: "*Loggerheads Rock 'n' Rule!*" "*Go Far — Go Carr*" "*Football is for Fun Lovers*" and "*Brotherly Bonds R Unbreakable.*"

He felt so lost. So confused. *How'd this happen? How'd I even get here?* He ruminated. Lights were on next door in Tripp's room. No game, no Tripp.

It grew chilly as the evening stretched on. Chase could hear the crowd cheer from behind him, through the woods. The lights of the stadium lit up the night, but didn't help his mood. It stayed dark. He thought Carr must be doing well from the cheers, but it was hard to tell.

He kept pouting. He hadn't gone to last year's game, because it was so far away. Now that he was on varsity, and the game was close enough to hear, he'd been suspended. Unjustly.

SO UNFAIR!

"Hey!"

The voice startled Chase. He sat quietly, waiting to see if he heard it again.

"Hey!" Chase recognized the voice. It was Tripp!

"Hey, yourself," he said, and looked over the side of the tree house. Tripp stood below, tossing his football up and down in his hand.

"Wanna throw?" Tripp asked.

"Sure!" and Chase scrambled down.

The woods were too dark, so they walked toward

Tripp's garage, where the outside floodlights lit up the driveway. They began throwing the ball, back and forth, back and forth. Neither boy spoke. Chase wanted to, but didn't want to spoil the moment. Everything he'd said to Tripp hadn't gone well, including earlier today. *Just keep playing catch*, he thought.

A big cheer. Really big. And then, silence. The game must have ended. But who won? Carr?

Tripp caught a pass and tucked the ball under his arm. "Thanks. I'm headed in. That's probably enough for tonight."

"Thanks," Chase called. "See ya, Thug," he added, but the door to Tripp's house had closed behind him.

Chase's mom and sister pulled in after a while and Hannah tiptoed into his darkened room. He always left the door open while he slept and wanted it to look natural. Chase was in bed, trying to look tired, but his heart was pounding.

"Chase. Chase. Are you awake?"

Chase rolled over toward her and tried to sound tired. "Yes. I'm awake."

"We won! You guys beat Pahokee!" Chase had been so focused on playing catch with Tripp that he'd nearly forgotten to ask.

"Yay!" But then his excitement faded as he remembered he'd been suspended from the team. Even so, he still found himself happy for his teammates.

"What was the score?"

"24 – 13. No, 24 – 14. I think. Something like that. Anyway, we won by a lot. It was really great!"

"Wow. So Roger must've played well," Chase said.

"He did. But I feel bad for him. He got hurt," Hannah said.

"What happened? How did we win if he was hurt? Who played quarterback?"

"It was right at the end," Hannah said. "The game was almost over and he got tackled and a couple of players had to help him off the field. It was something with his arm. His parents left the game and they told some other parents they were going to the hospital."

"Oh no. Poor Roger."

"But he played *great*, Chase. Really great. Everybody did," Hannah said.

"But who played quarterback after Roger?" Since Chase had been suspended hours before the game, Coach Skalaski wouldn't have had time for anyone else to practice. JB, Tripp, and Chase were all out. He couldn't think of who would be next to play quarterback for Carr.

Hannah shook her head. "I wasn't really paying attention to that. We all felt bad for Roger, and then all of a sudden, the game was over and we were celebrating." Chase nodded but still wondered.

"What'd you do while we were gone?" Hannah asked.

"Oh, you know. Hung around the house," Chase said.

He didn't mention Tripp, but he wasn't sure why. "Long day. I'm glad we won. I think I'll head to bed."

Hannah reached out and touched his hand. "I'm sorry you got suspended. I know you didn't cheat. Somehow, it'll turn out okay. I'm sure of it."

CHAPTER 22

Over the weekend, Chase and his mom brainstormed about how to get him cleared, but neither had any good ideas. They decided to talk to Mr. Sebring again next week. Chase hadn't heard a peep from Tripp since Friday night and was, once again, left with a sour stomach. He hoped that after tossing the ball around they'd have made some progress. How wrong that was! But before they could do anything Monday morning, Chase got a call from the school's office. He called his mom, "I don't know why, but Mr. Sebring asked that we meet him at the school at 11:00 am."

"Okay. Let me make some calls to reschedule things. I hope to be able to."

Chase looked at the clock. 9:50. His stomach began churning. "Please, Mom. You *have* to. I'm already in enough trouble about the math test."

Mrs. Clark sighed. Neither of them thought another meeting sounded like a good thing. More trouble. But she said, "I'll be there. I'll figure it out."

Chase was still worried when he and his mom entered Carr's front door and walked into the main office. Mr. Sebring's assistant, Ms. Louise, nodded them through the door. He couldn't tell if her look was friendly or not. *What in the world now*, he thought. Just when he and Tripp were at least talking again, a little, when this lousy month was starting to seem better … Now, he didn't know what was going on.

They entered Mr. Sebring's office and he was shocked to see Mr. and Mrs. Stevens. He looked around, his eyes finally settling on Tripp.

"Now what?" He felt sick. Tripp flashed a quick smile at him, then looked serious again.

Even so, Chase felt ready. He stood and started his defense.

He began to speak, articulately and confidently. He recited, "As surely as God lives, who has denied me justice, the Almighty, who has made my life bitter, as long as I have life within me, the breath of God in my nostrils, my lips will not say anything wicked, and my tongue will not utter lies."

Chase cleared his throat and continued, "I will never admit you are in the right; till I die, I will not deny my integrity. I will maintain my innocence and never let go of it; my conscience will not reproach me as long as I live."

Most of the adults in the room wore puzzlement on their faces as Chase's mom beamed with pride. "Um, will that be all, Chase?" asked Mr. Sebring.

Chase slumped back down into his chair and muttered, "Yeah, I memorized that last night. It's from Job 27." He looked over at Tripp. "It was his final word to his *friends*."

Mr. Sebring spoke. "Well-spoken, Chase. Chase and Mrs. Clark, we owe you both an apology. We have been told what happened on that test." He looked at Tripp. "It appears here that Tripp was the only one who cheated. Effective immediately, you've been reinstated to school and the football team, Chase.

"Tripp, you have not. You and I will still have to talk further."

Mr. Stevens spoke to Chase. "Tripp tells us that he's still having headaches, that they've never totally gone away from the night of the concussion." Tripp's parents looked older, Chase thought. Or at least more tired.

Tripp nodded. "It was fine the other night but it's killing me right now. It's better but it still comes and goes."

"And so," Mr. Sebring said, "we can't let him go back on the field. That's really the least of his worries. His parents are taking him to the doctor as soon as we finish here."

Tripp spoke. "So when we were taking that math test, I had no idea what was going on, Chase. No idea what the questions were asking me." Tripp looked unhappy. "In fact, that's why I sat behind you that day. I knew I couldn't pass the test. My memory has been shot by the concussion. I'm so sorry, Chase, that I got you in trouble. I had no idea how bad it would feel to lie about you."

Chase felt sick. And relieved. Now, he had proof, from a most unlikely source. Tripp himself.

"And, of course, since you had no idea either before, during, or after, about anything wrong happening on the test, your suspension is lifted, effective immediately," Mr. Sebring said. He then turned to Mrs. Clark. "Chase may go to practice right away, and will be eligible to play this week in the championship game."

Chase was ecstatic until he looked over at Tripp. His best friend would miss the game, and still wasn't well.

Coach Skalaski gathered the team on Tuesday afternoon. The state championship game was set for Saturday instead of Friday as usual, so he'd given them Monday off. Chase and JB were very glad for the extra day of rest. JB's ankle was a lot better. And Chase for being reinstated on Monday to school and not missing practice.

Now they were all glued to Coach's words.

"I wish we had an extra week to prepare, because Flagler is good and, of course, there is a lot riding on this game." Many of the players nodded. Coach looked around, then grinned.

"I'm just kidding! How many days does it take to get ready for a game?" he asked, and then answered his own question. "Three days! I learned that years ago. I don't care if it's the first game of the year, the state championship game against Flagler, or the Super Bowl. We've done it all year. *Three days.* It doesn't matter how big the game is, or how good the other team is. In truth, if we weren't playing them until next week, I'd give you this week off and we would practice three days next week."

Coach Skalaski seemed to be in a really good mood. Having JB back probably didn't hurt his outlook any.

Now the players were nodding vigorously.

"Guys, it's just another game. It really is, no matter what anyone might say. We're not going to play harder than we already have. We're not going to give 110 percent which would be freakish even if we could figure out a way to do it." He grinned, and a number of the guys laughed.

They had a great week of practice over the next three days. The guys were focused and healthy, with the exception of Roger Dalton. Roger had broken his right arm and had surgery Monday afternoon. Coach cut practice short on Wednesday afternoon and they headed on a bus to visit Roger at his house. He seemed his usual carefree self.

School was quieter since it was a short week,

Thanksgiving week, so Chase was able to spend time on homework again and the teachers were ready for a break too. So Chase was able to catch back up — in algebra and English. School was falling back into place, and his mom was pleased.

He'd waved at Tripp a couple of times across the yard on Thursday and Friday, but Tripp was in trouble with his parents — plus, he'd had a couple of doctor visits that week.

In the meantime, although he was calling it just another game, the state championship was obviously anything but just another game. Carr was facing the Flagler Engineers, from the East Coast of Florida, just south of St. Augustine. The school was named for Henry Flagler, who built railroads and hotels in Florida in the days before people thought to go to Florida for their vacations.

Back then, people thought of Florida as full of swamps and mosquitoes — which it was. Flagler made history by connecting his railroad across the water all the way down to Key West. And after that, vacationers started traveling to the state.

The Flagler Engineers were also setting records, just like Henry Flagler had. They were 13 – 0 and *USA Today* called them the number three team in the entire nation. Their quarterback, Luke Whittemore, was headed to Duke after he graduated, choosing them over scholarship offers from every other major college in the country. Flagler had a *lot* of great players. Definitely not just another game, no matter what Coach said. In addition, the game was being played at Jacksonville Stadium, home of the Jacksonville Destroyers.

Coach Skalaski truly believed that his main mission at Carr was to teach his players about life. At the same time, he wanted to win. Badly. He wanted that first state championship for Carr. They were *so close* and might not ever get this close again. The ball might not bounce the right way, and they had caught a break when Raines had lost to Cocoa Beach in the opening round. Most importantly, their senior quarterback, James Brown, was a once-in-a-lifetime player. Coach Skalaski figured that he'd probably never coach a player that good again.

Of course, the once-in-a-lifetime player hadn't touched a football in over a week. Plus, the coaches had to decide: in a game this big, could their backup quarterback *really* be an eighth-grader?

Thursday afternoon after Chase had eaten turkey at his house, he was at Carr for practice. Coach Skalaski called Chase into his office before practice; all the coaches were sitting in there. They had all been debating the question for several days, of who should be the backup quarterback.

Coach asked Chase if he thought he was up to the job, to be the backup quarterback with Roger hurt.

"Of course, Coach. I know all the plays."

Coach thanked him and Chase left. And gulped. Could he really do it? *Of course.* What would they decide?

Minutes later, Coach Skalaski stood next to Chase at practice and spoke quietly. "In addition to knowing the Scout Team the way you do, I need you to also take a few snaps with our offense."

Chase nodded and his pulse raced.

"You've done a fine job all year, but if for some reason you are playing for us on Saturday night, we're going to keep it very simple. We're going to run *Power Right* and *Power Left* and merely hand the ball off. Nice and simple. You are going to manage the huddle and manage the team for us. Nothing fancy."

Coach Skalaski called the team together to start practice on Friday afternoon, and announced that Chase would be their backup. "He's earned it. Hopefully we won't need him — after all, JB is our guy. But if we do, Chase is our guy. We'll just have him hand-off and hopefully JB would be able to come back in. After all, this is why we had the JV run the same plays as the varsity, so that someone like Chase could step right in and do great — which he will if we need him."

Chase felt grateful indeed. His heart swelled with pride. He was so ready for this!

Coach Skalaski scheduled a light practice for Friday

afternoon. When Chase arrived at the locker room, he found a sign on the locker room door: "Dress in your game uniforms for a team photo. Tennis shoes, no pads."

Along with his teammates, he dressed accordingly and headed outside for a team picture in front of their stadium. After twenty minutes of fidgeting, the photographer said they were finally finished, and the boys walked toward the practice field.

They found a bus waiting for them, and climbed on. Coach Skalaski was waiting on board and announced that instead of practice, they were going bowling!

Offense against defense!

The boys were naturally competitive, but had fun along the way. Everyone laughed a lot at the Kingstons. Will decided to play with the defense, since he sometimes played defensive end, along with offensive line. Chris yelled "Traitor!" every time Will was about to release the ball, and by the end, Chase and all of the offense was yelling it.

The defense won anyway. Even if Will didn't bowl well that day.

Two hours later, they were dropped back off at school, the defense happy in their victory. Actually, everyone was happy.

And tomorrow was the game.

CHAPTER 23

The state championship game kickoff was scheduled for 7:00 pm, but Coach Skalaski had the players depart Carr at 2:00 pm. The drive was only forty minutes to the Jacksonville Destroyers stadium, and Coach Skalaski wanted the players to have plenty of time to get used to the field, the locker room, and the size of the stadium.

When they gathered at Carr, there were four River County school buses to meet them, because the band and cheerleaders were also going. A fifth bus — a spirit bus — was also taking Carr students, but was not leaving until later that afternoon. Parents and students were gathered in the parking lot, and had decorated the buses in blue and green.

After a spirited sendoff with lots of cheering, and a short and uneventful ride, the players walked off the bus and through statues of sailors and Navy fighter planes outside of the stadium. Because of the two Navy bases in Jacksonville, the team had been named the Destroyers and the stadium was covered in Navy themes.

They walked through a plain gray door and down a hallway to their locker room. A few of the players, like Tripp and Chase, had seen a professional locker room, but most hadn't. They were in awe. Coach was glad he'd gotten there early. They definitely needed a little time to get used to it and work the butterflies out of their systems.

"I'm headed out to the field," JB said to Chase. "Want to come?" Chase was sitting in the large wood locker, with his white jersey and blue helmet hung neatly from hooks and his blue pants folded on the bench of his locker and looked up. He nodded and followed JB down the tunnel to the field.

They walked around on the grass for a few minutes. "Did you notice?" JB finally asked.

"Notice what? No," answered Chase.

"That it's just like our field. Same grass, same size field. Sure, the grass is a little nicer and the stands a lot bigger, but the field is the same." JB grinned and Chase nodded. He hadn't thought about it, but it made sense. Same field. Same game.

As they left the field to head back into the tunnel, three men walked alongside them up into the tunnel.

Chase recognized one, Keith Kushner, the head coach of the Destroyers.

Wow!

JB smiled and introduced himself to each, then introduced Chase. They introduced themselves as Coach Kushner, Michael Smith, and Jim Trotter, and JB said how much he enjoyed their work. They asked him about the state championship game and after talking all the way back to the locker room, they parted and headed in the other direction toward the Destroyers' offices.

"Who were those other guys?" Chase asked.

"One was Jim Trotter, who writes about professional football for *Sports Illustrated*."

"Cool," Chase said. He looked back down the hall as they turned a corner.

"And the other is Michael Smith of ESPN. He'll be broadcasting the Destroyers' game this week. They're both in town getting ready for the Monday night football game here. The Destroyers are playing the Cleveland Rockers on Monday night."

"That's really cool. I would've never known who they were although Michael Smith did seem familiar — I guess from watching football on television."

Although Chase thought that time would take forever to pass, before long he was dressed and heading out for warmups. As Coach had told them, Flagler looked intimidating in their crimson and gold uniforms. And fast. After glancing their way, Chase decided to ignore Flagler and focus on his passes and handoffs. He couldn't help himself, though. He would glance at Flagler, or up into the upper deck or giant scoreboard. JB said it was the same size field and everything, but *wow*. The whole thing was *amazing*.

Before he knew it, warmups were over and they headed back into the locker room for the last pre-game talk of the season.

As he headed into the tunnel, he heard his name. "Chase! Megan! Look up!" came the shouts. He looked up and saw his sister and friends at the wall, waving. Hannah, Kate, his mom, and even Mark Plazas and Ken and Tracy Block were all standing at the wall, smiling and waving.

And Tripp!

"Hey y'all!" Chase called, and to Tripp he yelled, "Wish you were down here!"

Tripp smiled, nodded, and yelled, "Another time! Next year!"

Chase beamed and trotted into the tunnel. He felt great. It didn't matter now what happened in the game. Almost.

"Lady and Gentlemen, I only have two things to say. First, have fun." Coach Skalaski smiled. "This should be *fun*." Then the smile faded a little. "And the other thing is to keep playing hard. We may get bad calls or bad breaks. They may jump out to an early lead. Whatever happens, keep playing hard. Keep fighting."

Minutes later, Carr was coming out of the tunnel to the roar of the crowd. It didn't fill the 70,000 seat stadium, not by a long shot, but it was the largest crowd they'd played in front of. Ever. Far bigger than Lake Butler. Chase expected to be nervous, but instead found himself excited.

He stood at attention with his helmet under his arm and hand over his heart as the National Anthem was sung, and then ducked when four Navy fighter planes raced just over the top of the stadium. It was deafening, and the entire crowd was cheering. Chase got goosebumps. He'd seen flyovers from the local Navy bases and plenty of Jacksonville Destroyer games, but one for *their* game?!

Coach Skalaski had told them that JB and the Kingston twins were the team captains for the game, but he hadn't told them that Roger would be there as well. Roger surprised them by joining the other three and walking out to midfield with his sling. Roger called the flip of the coin — "Tails" — and when the referee said that it came up tails, the Carr crowd cheered. The Loggerheads would get the ball to start the game!

Flagler's kick was high and deep, and Jacob Kaplan caught it at the 5-yard line and started running up the field.

Boom! He was tackled at the 12-yard line.

Chase heard shouts of "Ball! Ball!" coming from the

Flagler players and after the pile cleared, the referee pointed: Flagler ball.

Jacob fumbled, and Flagler recovered at Carr's 12-yard line.

Two plays later, Flagler punched it in for the TD, getting on the board, 7 – 0. Coach Skalaski was right. Flagler started fast. The Loggerheads needed to hang in there.

Flagler kicked off again, but this time, instead of kicking it deep to Jacob again, they onside kicked! The ball bounced ten yards and was recovered by a Flagler player before any Carr players could get to it. Once again, Flagler had the football!

Coach Skalaski had said to stay calm but his own face had turned red. Flagler had kicked off twice already, but JB and the Carr offense hadn't touched the ball at all.

Carr's defense was able to stop Flagler, and JB and the offense finally did get the ball.

JB passed and ran equally well on that first drive, leading Carr down the field. On third down with three yards to go from Flagler's 13-yard line, JB fumbled the snap. Fortunately, he was able to fall on the ball and keep it. Megan trotted on the field and coolly kicked a field goal. JB's little sister cut Flagler's lead to 7 – 3.

JB came off the field and grinned at Chase when he reached the sideline. With Roger hurt and unable to play, JB was now holding for his sister on field goals, like they'd done in the backyard so many times.

"That was awful," he said. Chase realized JB was talking about the fumble, and despite the grin, he was upset.

"We're on the board," Chase said. "Focus on the good, forget the bad." JB nodded. Chase could tell he'd just needed a simple reminder.

Megan kicked off and the two teams exchanged punts to finish the first quarter.

Flagler scored on a long touchdown pass by their great quarterback, Whittemore, when a Carr player slipped. Now it was 14 – 3, and there were only six minutes until halftime.

Flagler had the ball once again, and if they scored again before halftime, things would look pretty bleak for Carr.

On the second play for Flagler, Whittemore threw a pass that was tipped and intercepted by Jackson Parker! Jackson began weaving through the Flagler players toward the end zone and was finally tackled after he'd returned the interception all the way to the Flagler 6-yard line!

Right before the second quarter ended, JB scored on a touchdown run and Carr trailed 14 – 10. It was a huge turning point for the Loggerheads.

CHAPTER 24

The players spread out in the big locker room and rested, eating orange slices and drinking green Gatorade. Chase couldn't find purple.

Moments later, one of the referees stuck his head in the locker room and looked toward Coach Skalaski. "Coach, you've got thirty seconds left 'til you've gotta come out."

Coach Skalaski nodded and gathered them together.

"Guys, great job. Megan, great kicks. Sure enough, they started fast and got ahead of us. But we're tough. And now we're right in the game!"

The players charged out of the locker room and back onto the field as the fans cheered. It felt like the whole town of Lincoln was there, but Flagler had just as many fans. The stadium was really loud.

Because Carr had chosen to receive the kickoff to

start the game after Roger won the toss, Flagler got the ball first to start the second half. They took it on a long, slow drive and scored a touchdown but missed the extra point.

20 – 10, Flagler. The defensive players for Carr trotted off the field, slowly. They were getting tired.

Unfortunately for them, there was good news and bad news. The good news was that JB scored a touchdown on a long run and Carr was only behind 20 – 17! The bad news was that because it happened very quickly, they didn't get much of a rest before they had to get back on the field.

The defense rallied, though, and stopped the Flagler offense.

The teams exchanged punts. The third quarter turned into the fourth, and time was slipping away.

JB's face was hard, focused. Coach Skalaski stayed calm, keeping the boys calm. But there was a growing anxiety on the sideline; Chase could feel it. Carr punted once again.

Flagler slowly drove down the field to Carr's 5-yard line. Chase held his breath. There was under two minutes left, and with Flagler already leading, 20 – 17, a touchdown would ice the win for Flagler.

On third down, Coach Skalaski gambled by calling an all-out blitz, and Will Kingston was able to get to Luke Whittemore and sack him before he could get rid of the ball!

It was fourth down from Carr's 12-yard line, and Flagler was forced to kick a field goal.

23 – 17, Flagler.

Just as important as the score, the time on the clock dwindled. Carr would be getting the ball with a chance to win the game, but only fifty seconds remained. They *had* to score.

Jacob Kaplan caught the kickoff at Carr's 1-yard line and took off, weaving and dodging until he was tackled twenty-nine yards later on their own 30-yard line. A good kickoff return, but only forty seconds remained in the game. Carr had only one time-out left to use to stop the clock.

JB caught the shotgun snap and rolled out to his right, toward the Flagler sideline. He was waiting for a receiver to get open but none did. He was finally tackled by a diving Flagler player who hit JB's legs low and flipped the big quarterback out of bounds. Chase had seen a lot of players tackle JB low — he was so broad that many defensive players didn't want to try to hit JB up high, around the shoulders.

The clock stopped with twenty-nine seconds left to play, leaving the ball still at the Carr 30-yard line. No gain.

Chase could see that JB was having trouble getting up. Finally JB stood and limped back to the middle of the field, but then sat down in a heap. Oh no! His ankle was hurt again!

Todd, the trainer, ran onto the field to help JB while Coach Skalaski ran over to Chase. "Chase, get in there!" Chase started to put his helmet on and trot out, but Coach called, "Wait!"

Chase came back to Coach. "Chase, we can't just hand the ball off. I know that was our plan for you, but there's not enough time."

Coach looked over Chase's shoulder and saw that JB was walking off with Todd. JB's leg seemed better, but once the referee had called an injury time-out, the hurt player had to sit out for one play.

Chase was still going in. "We're going to run *Trio RightGun 200 Throwback*."

Chase gulped. He hadn't thrown a pass in over two hours, since pregame warmups. And he hadn't run that play since the JV team had lost to the Raiders two months before.

He thought of the prayer with JB behind the locker room, and thought, *Anything is possible, especially when it comes to football.*

And then he remembered a favorite piece of Scripture from Philippians 4:13: *I can do all this through him who gives me strength.* He decided that would be the one he'd repeat, like the way Megan always repeated Psalm 23 before a kick.

Coach made sure that four receivers were in the game and Dimitri, Carson, and Jacob lined up to the right while Drew lined up left. Chase got in the huddle and called the play: "*Trio RightGun 200 Throwback*, on two." They clapped, broke the huddle, and Chase stood in the shotgun and called out the cadence:

"*Blue 17, Blue 17, hut, hut!*"

The biggest moment of his life. He had to go with "*Blue 17.*"

Chase caught the snap and rolled to his right, toward the trio of receivers. He gave Drew time to run the *Post Route* and Drew was about to make the cut to the *Corner Route* when Chase heard the voice.

"Look out!"

Chase heard Tripp's voice above the roar of the crowd. Maybe he didn't actually hear it *above* the crowd, but just *through* it. Best friends were like that—Chase would know Tripp's voice anywhere.

Defensive end from behind, Chase thought.

He didn't even look, he just stopped rolling to his right and ducked. The Flagler defensive end sailed over Chase's head! Chase stood back up and threw back to his left to Drew, as far as he could throw the ball.

Drew caught it over a leaping Flagler player! He ran toward the end zone but was tackled at the Flagler 8-yard line!

Chase was jumping up and down, celebrating the play, then looked toward the sideline. Coach Skalaski was waving at him, frantically signaling for a time-out. Chase turned toward the referee and put his hands in the shape of a capital "T."

Time-out!

Three seconds left.

JB came back onto the field and high-fived Chase as the eighth-grader ran off to the sideline.

"Nice job," JB said, and grinned. He didn't look like he was feeling any pressure. Chase saw his lips move and realized JB had borrowed Megan's mantra: "The Lord is my shepherd. The Lord is my shepherd. The Lord ..."

With no timeouts and only three seconds, this would be the final play. It all hung on this one play—Carr would either lose the game or tie for the state championship if they could score a touchdown.

JB took the snap and rolled out to his left, looking for an open receiver. There were none. A Flagler defender hit him, but the big quarterback shook him off like a plastic chew toy and kept running.

Another defender tried, another defender fell to the ground.

JB kept running, now straight up the field toward the end zone. At the 3-yard line, a Flagler player decided to dive at JB's legs. JB leapt over him as if he was running the hurdles, landing in the end zone!

Touchdown!

23 – 23!

With no time left in regulation, Carr was allowed to try the extra point. Megan ran onto the field and calmly kicked the ball straight through the uprights, just like always.

Carr Loggerheads 24, Flagler Engineers 23.

Carr High School was the state champions!

The players celebrated with each other and the coaches. Coach Skalaski was crying, hugging his wife. Coach P was holding Elise ("Kickoff") out on the field. Then they tried to calm down enough to be good sports while shaking hands with the disappointed Flagler players. Luke Whittemore walked over to Chase. "Nice throw," he said. Chase thanked him and the Flagler quarterback slowly walked off the field.

Chase hugged Coach Skalaski, Megan, the Kingstons, and everyone nearby. He felt like a hero. They all did. He turned and looked into the stands toward the place where he'd seen Hannah, Kate, Tripp, and the Blocks. There were the girls, along with his mom and grand-parents. But he didn't see Tripp. *Where was Tripp?*

"I'm right here." Tripp could tell he was looking for him and gave him a hug. "Not a bad throw for a scrawny guy." They laughed.

"Or a thug."

They laughed again.

JB walked over and gave them both a big, sweaty hug. "And the good news — basketball practice starts next week! And nothing bad happens in basketball!"

DISCUSSION QUESTIONS FOR SNAP DECISION

1. The students at Carr voted to change the mascot to Loggerheads. Are team names just for fun, or can they have other value too? Can they be harmful?

2. Coach Skalaski suspended the players who skipped school for an entire game, even though the players who skipped the previous year only did extra running (and didn't miss a game). Was that fair? Should he want to be "fair"?

3. Tripp was glad that Chase, his best friend, spent so much time with Tripp and his dad. But there was also a part of Tripp that was jealous of Chase's

time with Tripp's dad. He asked Chase in chapter 17, " ... did you come here to see my *dad*?" Were you surprised by that question? Should Tripp's dad have handled things differently?

4. Treatment for concussions has changed over time as knowledge of the brain has grown. As recently as 2009, treatment for concussions included keeping the patient in a dark room, not letting them read or watch television, all in an attempt to keep the brain still and quiet. Now treatment includes trying to use the brain — in limited amounts — the way that we would rehab another injured body part. What are other ways in which our scientific knowledge has changed recently?

5. Chase's football season would have been less stressful if he hadn't told the truth about Tripp. Did he do the right thing? Are there times when lying would be okay?

6. Why did Coach Skalaski take the team to visit the Archie Carr National Wildlife Refuge, Pahokee, and Lake Okeechobee? Is there a value to visiting different places?

7. JB is a role model for Chase, even before Chase gets to know him. Is it important to have a role model? Does it matter if we have a "good" role model? How can we make sure that we choose a good one?

8. Hannah keeps having nightmares. Why do you think she has them? If you were Chase, what would you do to help her?

9. Does a role model always have to be someone older? What about when JB starts copying his little sister by repeating the 23rd Psalm when he takes the field ... is she a role model for him?

10. Coach Skalaski doesn't yell at his players. Is it possible to be a good coach without yelling? Why do so many coaches do it?

11. Mo Isom told the kids to find out "who God made you to be." What does that mean? But what if God made you different than everybody else?

GLOSSARY

Audible—verbal play change by the quarterback during the cadence

Barnburner—an exciting, close game (usually one with lots of scoring)

Blindside—the back side of the quarterback

Buzzsaw—a team that is playing really well and "cuts" right through the opposition

Cadence—verbal calls a quarterback uses to signal the center when to snap the ball and begin the play

Down—the football word for "a play." In American football, teams have four downs to move the ball forward at least ten yards in order to keep possession of the football.

Extra point—a field goal that occurs after a touchdown, and is worth one point.

Field Goal — after being snapped, the ball is placed on the ground and an offensive plays kicks it. If it goes through the uprights, it is worth three points (a field goal).

First Down — moving the ball forward at least ten yards over the course of four downs results in four "new" downs for the offense, so that the count is reset to "first down"

Free Safety — the safety lined up on the opposite side of the field as the tight end

Gridiron — nickname for a football field

Kickoff — After every score, the ball is placed on a tee and the scoring team kicks the ball to the other team. At the start of the game, the team to kickoff is determined by a coin flip. At the start of the second half, whichever team kicked off to start the game will "receive" the second half kickoff, regardless of any other kickoffs that may have taken place in the first half.

O-Line — nickname for the five offensive line positions (Left Tackle, Left Guard, Center, Right Guard, Right Tackle)

Playbook — a team's diagrams and descriptions of its plays

Punt — to kick the ball to the defense when a team believes that it will not be able to successfully gain ten yards during its four downs (punts usually occur on fourth down)

Red Zone — the twenty-yard area on a football field between the twenty-yard line and the goal line

Sack — to tackle the quarterback behind the line of scrimmage

Safety — a defensive player lined up in the rear of the defensive formation, usually the farthest person from the ball, as a last line of defense ("Safety" can also refer to tackling an offensive player with the ball in their own end zone, resulting in two points for the defense.)

Scout team — the players that simulate the opposing team during practice

Shotgun snap — when the center snaps the ball through the air to the quarterback standing several steps behind him (instead of the usual snap with the quarterback's hands under the center so that the ball is handed directly from the center to quarterback)

Special teams — those players or plays that are involved with any of the "kicking" plays (punts, kickoffs, field goals and extra points)

Two-point conversion — instead of kicking an extra point after a touchdown, a team can choose to run a play from the three-yard line (in high school). If they successfully cross the goal line, the play is worth two points.

UNDERSTANDING CONCUSSION

SOME COMMON SYMPTOMS

Headache	Fogginess
Pressure in the Head	Grogginess
Nausea/Vomiting	Poor Concentration
Dizziness	Memory Problems
Balance Problems	Confusion
Double Vision	"Feeling Down"
Blurry Vision	Not "Feeling Right"
Sensitive to Light	Feeling Irritable
Sensitive to Noise	Slow Reaction Time
Sluggishness	Sleep Problems
Haziness	

WHAT IS A CONCUSSION?

A concussion is a type of traumatic brain injury that changes the way the brain normally works. A concussion is caused by a fall, bump, blow, or jolt to the head or body that causes the head and brain to move quickly back and forth. A concussion can be caused by a shaking, spinning, or a sudden stopping and starting of the head. Even a "ding," "getting your bell rung," or what seems to be a mild bump or blow to the head can be serious. A concussion can happen even if you haven't been knocked out.

You can't see a concussion. Signs and symptoms of concussions can show up right after the injury or may not appear or be noticed until days or weeks after the injury. If you notice symptoms, seek medical attention right away. You should not return to play on the day of the injury and until a health care professional says you are okay to return to play.

IF YOU SUSPECT A CONCUSSION:

1. SEEK MEDICAL ATTENTION RIGHT AWAY. A health care professional will be able to decide how serious the concussion is and when it is safe for you to return to regular activities, including sports. Don't hide it, report it. Ignoring symptoms and trying to "tough it out" often makes it worse.

2. STAY OUT OF YOUR GAMES. Concussions take time to heal. Don't return to play the day of injury and until a health care professional says it's okay. If you return to play too soon, while the brain is still healing, you risk a greater chance of having a second concussion. In fact, young children and teens are more likely to get a concussion and take longer to recover than adults. Repeat or second concussions increase the time it takes to recover and can be very serious. They can cause permanent brain damage, affecting you for a lifetime. They can be fatal. It is better to miss one game than the whole season.

3. TELL THE SCHOOL ABOUT ANY PREVIOUS CONCUSSION. Schools should know if you had a previous concussion. Your school may not know about a concussion received in another sport or activity unless you notify them.

CONCUSSION DANGER SIGNS:

In rare cases, a dangerous blood clot may form on the brain in a person with a concussion and crowd the brain against the skull. You should receive immediate medical attention if after a bump, blow, or jolt to the head or body you exhibit any of the following danger signs:

- One pupil larger than the other
- Feel drowsy or cannot be awakened

- Have a headache that gets worse
- Weakness, numbness, or decreased coordination
- Repeated vomiting or nausea
- Slurred speech
- Convulsions or seizures
- Cannot recognize people/places
- Become increasingly confused, restless, or agitated
- Have unusual behavior
- Lose consciousness (Even a brief loss of consciousness should be taken seriously.)

HOW TO RESPOND TO A REPORT OF A CONCUSSION:

If you report one or more symptoms of a concussion after a bump, blow, or jolt to the head or body, you should be kept out of athletic play the day of the injury. You should only return to play with permission from a health care professional experienced in evaluating for concussion. During recovery, rest is key. Exercising or activities that involve a lot of concentration (such as studying, working on the computer, or playing video games) may cause concussion symptoms to reappear or get worse. People who return to school after a concussion may need to spend fewer hours at school, take rest breaks, be given extra help and time, spend less time reading, writing or on a computer. After a concussion, returning to sports and school is a gradual process that should be monitored by a health care professional.

Remember: Concussion affects people differently. While most people with a concussion recover quickly and fully, some will have symptoms that last for days, or even weeks. A more serious concussion can last for months or longer.

To learn more, go to www.cdc.gov/concussion.

Sources: Michigan Department of Community Health, CDC and the National Operating Committee on Standards for Athletic Equipment (NOCSAE)

AUTHOR'S NOTE:

I was warned that the transition to writing a work of fiction would be laborious. I didn't believe the warnings.

I was wrong.

So wrong, that during the process, I found myself taking solace in a note from my youngest daughter, Ellie, stating "Dad is a terrific writer!" and in my oldest daughter, Hannah, who kept saying, "I really like the story." Between the girls and my wife, who always thinks that I'll figure it out, we gutted through it.

The other thing that made it so challenging was tackling—see what I did there?—the topic of concussions that is so timely, scary, and shifting with new information, that I wanted to handle it appropriately and fairly.

In trying to accomplish all that, I needed help.

I'm grateful to so many who did so along the way, including the team at Zondervan. Kim Childress had great ideas to keep prodding me along, and Kelly White was a terrific editor in her assistance of Kim. Molly Lauryssens's suggestions kept the story moving, and all three helped keep my written transgressions from making it into the final product. Annette Bourland never lost faith, and Sara Merritt and Nan Snow helped make it all a reality.

Coach Cummings, Jake Dahl, Iim Higgins, and Neil Lauryssens kept my football and algebra on the straight and narrow.

Ken and Tracy Block, Kris Carter, Chase and Cindy Clark, Mike Garafolo, Mo Isom, Brian Kaplan, Peter King, John Kingston, Keith Kushner, Scott MacLean, Mark Plazas, Damon Preston, Charlie Skalaski, Michael Smith, Jim Trotter, Alan Williams, Carey and Ellen Wood, thanks for the names.

Dave Werner at the University of Florida taught me so much about concussions and the evolving knowledge of treating brain injuries that I ... well, I understood so little that I hope I didn't mess it up in the telling.

Jeff Parker, head football coach at Eastside High School, my alma mater, and Mark Whittemore, head football coach at Buchholz High School (my wife's alma mater), were gracious with their time and expertise and opening up their practices to me, since it's been a long time since I was in high school. A long time. I don't like it when you guys play each other.

Charles Martin, you're a far better writer than I am, and I appreciate you telling me to keep pressing on, even when I worried that I was off base.

Mom and Dad, thanks for your support.

James Brown, thanks for being you.

Tony Dungy, for telling a publisher, years ago, that "either this book happens with Nathan (who, admittedly, has never written a book) or it doesn't happen." A whole new world of possibilities for me as a result of your (blind?) faith.

As always, DJ Snell of Legacy, LLC, for shepherding me through this process. Part agent, part counselor. No really: part agent, part counselor.

The penultimate and antepenultimate thanks go to Hannah and Ellie Kate, for sharing me with the demanding book-writing process. You two make everyday life so fun, along with Mom.

And finally, my darling Amy, thanks for your belief in me when there was no tangible reason to believe.

Any mistakes in the telling of this story are mine alone. The people above told me better but I misunderstood. It's not their fault. Well, it is, but I'm trying to be gracious.

NW